THE GREEK'S
Stowaway Bride

THE GREEK'S
Stowaway Bride

ALEXIA ADAMS

Entangled Publishing, LLC
10940 S Parker Rd
Suite 327
Parker, CO 80134
rights@entangledpublishing.com

Indulgence is an imprint of Entangled Publishing, LLC.

Edited by Alethea Spiridon Hopson
Cover design by LJ Anderson/Mayhem Cover Creations
Cover art from kiuikson and tepic/Deposit Photos

Manufactured in the United States of America

First Edition November 2015

I dedicate this book to the people of Greece and Egypt.

Chapter One

Demetri clutched the wall as the boat suddenly changed momentum. He'd paid five million euros to have the yacht custom built. If it had broken down already, there'd be hell to pay. Perhaps the captain had noticed something in the water or it was a routine check of the new engine. Demetri would investigate right after he had his shower.

The cool spray felt wonderful after his intense workout in the onboard gym. He turned the showerhead to massage and let the water pummel his back. Three entire days with no meetings, no urgent emails or other obligations meant absolute bliss. Just him and the sea, and a dedicated crew to cater to his every whim.

As soon as they docked at his birth island of Gavdos the peace would end. He was going to propose to Christina who lived there, and then there would be a flurry of wedding plans to contend with. The rings were in the next room waiting for the perfect moment to slip on her slender finger. He hadn't decided whether they should marry right away and get all the wedding nonsense over and done with quickly. Or perhaps he'd suggest a long engagement so it annoyed him in small doses. Christina was biddable and would do whatever he decided.

The sooner he married, though, the sooner he'd be able to put in an offer on the beach property in direct sight of his grandfather's house. The seller insisted the land go to a married couple. Once it was in his name, however, there'd be no stopping his plans to develop it into a luxury resort. Then each morning when his grandfather looked out the window, he'd have to acknowledge that the bastard grandson he despised had made it in life, that Demetri had made something of the family name rather than disgrace it, as his grandfather maintained.

He closed his eyes and imagined the happiness on his mother's face when he was finally able to provide her with a standard of living worthy of her devotion to him. She'd refused to move with him to Crete and instead insisted on staying on the tiny island of Gavdos with her parents. She'd refused even to let him build her a beautiful house there, but once his resort was up and running, he'd insist that she take one of the opulent bungalows he envisaged. He might have to come up with some excuse as to why he needed her to live on-site. It was time she had her own place where she could do what she wanted rather than have to answer to his tyrannical grandfather.

His eyes snapped open as the bathroom door clicked open and then closed again. He blinked. Holy hotness, this cruise just got interesting. A beautiful woman he'd never seen before stood in the room. Her long dark hair was carefully draped down her front, obscuring her body, but he'd bet his new boat she was naked.

Before he could ask what she wanted, she opened the shower door and stepped inside. She took a deep breath, held his gaze, and then wrapped her arms around his torso. Her body pressed against his—full, soft breasts crushed against his upper abdomen. Only her damp hair prevented their skin from touching.

"What the?" He opened his mouth to ask the question again in Greek, but she stood on tiptoe and whispered into his ear.

"Please. Help me. My name is Rania—"

A millisecond later the bathroom door flung open and two men dressed in black leveled automatic weapons at him. Rather than screaming, the woman in his arms pulled his head down and kissed him. He blinked again. No, there was definitely a naked woman in his shower and two heavily armed men in the bathroom. Was he being pranked with a scene out of a James Bond film? Any moment now someone would yell, "Gotcha!" and he'd discover he was the next YouTube sensation. Who would dare pull such a trick on him?

Rania released his lips but clung to him, her head buried in his neck. Her body trembled but whether from the kiss, which had been intense, or the situation, he didn't know. Time to find out.

"Get out!" he bellowed, although which of the intruders would respond he didn't care. Rania had spoken English so he kept to that language. She tightened her arms around his waist, and he glanced down at her. Her almond-colored eyes were huge and tinged with fear. He could be holding a terrorist about to blow his boat to smithereens. However, she was a hell of a lot more alluring than the two men with their machine guns.

One of the black clad men lowered his weapon a fraction. "You have one minute before we come back and start shooting," he said in heavily accented English. He spoke to the man next to him in Arabic, and they backed out of the room leaving the door ajar.

Rania dropped her arms and tried to step away from him.

Damn if he wasn't holding her as tightly as she had been him. He released her, and she quickly opened the shower door then wrapped herself in one of the towels. She handed the other to him, keeping her eyes averted from his lower half in a belated display of modesty. As he secured the towel around his waist she grabbed his hand and then pulled open the bathroom door. Before he'd even stepped fully into the room, Rania began to yell at the two men in Arabic, her gestures so wild her towel almost came loose. Demetri smiled at the confusion on the faces of the armed men, until one raised his gun again.

"Speak in English," Demetri demanded. It was his boat after all; he had a right to know what was going on.

Rania turned to him and shot a devastating smile his direction. "*Habibi*, I was explaining to these … men … that we are on our honeymoon. They have no right to board our boat and point their guns at us."

Maybe it was the guns. Maybe he'd already met his quota of shocks for the day. Maybe he was actually having an aneurysm and imagining all this. Whatever the cause, he didn't react to the word "honeymoon" or its implication. He addressed the men. "Who are you and what do you want?"

"We are *friends* of the Egyptian government. This woman is related to an enemy of the people of Egypt. We are here to take her into custody."

Rania took his hand in hers and squeezed it tight, shifting her body so it fit against his side.

"We are in Greek waters, on a boat registered in Greece. You have no authority here," Demetri said. "My captain will have alerted the Hellenic Coast Guard that you have illegally boarded my boat. I'm sure you know who I am. Do you really want to start an international incident? Because you will have to kill me before I let you take my wife." He didn't even hesitate on the last word and moved to shelter Rania further with his body.

Both men lowered their guns and had a rapid discussion in Arabic. Their gazed darted between him and Rania. Finally, the taller gunman said, "We have not heard of this wedding. Do you have any proof of this marriage?"

Shit.

"Yes, I have our marriage certificate here," Rania shocked him by saying. She released his hand and moved over to the bedside table. He looked around. Ten minutes ago, when he'd walked through to take a shower, the stateroom had been immaculate. The bed made so tightly he could have bounced on it without wrinkling the top sheet. Now the blankets were tossed aside, the sheets askew, and three empty condom wrappers littered the floor, not to mention the trail of clothes from the door to the bed, his and he assumed, Rania's. A black bra with red lace dangled from the lamp beside the sofa. A see-through, red G-string hung precariously from the handle to the walk-in wardrobe. Someone had had a hell of a good time in this room. Too bad it hadn't been him.

Rania handed a paper to the first gunman who seemed to be in charge. "It's in Albanian. I'm sure that's not an issue for you," she said, her voice overly sweet. The men perused it carefully, even holding it up to the light as though checking for authenticity.

While they examined the document, Demetri studied Rania. He searched his memory for where he could have met her before but came up blank, and he would have remembered a woman as beautiful as her. Her long dark hair, which she'd freed from the towel, fell in wet strands to her waist. Thick, black lashes framed light-brown, amber-flecked eyes. She bit down on her lower lip for a second, and the desire generated by her earlier kiss flooded to his groin again. She'd tasted as good as she looked. But she was a complete stranger. He'd been in Albania on business for four days before he'd taken possession of his new yacht in Pireus for its maiden voyage. The trip had been interesting, but he was pretty sure he'd have remembered getting married. He'd visited several potential sites in Albania, considering them for his hotel portfolio. It was a gamble if the Balkan country could be the next great tourist destination. With unrest in North Africa and the Middle East, adventurous tourists were searching for a new destination—luxury off the beaten track, and he would be the one to provide it to them.

"Why did you marry in Albania and not in Greece?" The first gunman's abrupt question brought Demetri back to the bizarre situation.

"That is none of your business," Rania said. For a second her hand fluttered to her stomach, implying their quick wedding was rooted in a possible unplanned pregnancy. Without saying anything else, she crossed her arms over her chest and glared at the men. Despite the seriousness of the situation, and he still wasn't sure if he was safe with this woman, he admired her courage and spunk in standing up to the gunmen. If sweet, gentle Christina were here, she'd be in a flood of tears, hiding behind him, not defying two heavily armed men to see through her web of lies.

Another conference ensued in Arabic between the two men. For a moment Rania relaxed then tensed again when the second man said something.

"We will stay aboard to ensure you are truly married, and that Mrs. Christodoulou does not get off the boat and try to make her way to Egypt."

"That is not acceptable," Demetri said.

The guns raised again. "It is not open for discussion."

A smart man knew when he was out-gunned. "The Greek authorities will remove you both from my boat. Until then, get out of my room and allow my wife to dress. She's getting cold."

Rania gave an exaggerated shiver as if to back up his words. Both men left the room but the leader said before closing the door, "We will be waiting outside. Do not do anything stupid."

• • •

Rania let out a huge, silent sigh. Out of the frying pan, into the fire. At least this fire was heated with one intensely hot man. Even naked, Demetri Christodoulou exuded power. Attach a couple of electrodes to him and he could light up her Christmas tree. Every one of his many muscles was honed to perfection, his lips full and firm, his dark eyes piercing, his jaw chiseled and strong. Yup, he was genuine and the only thing currently standing between her and disappearing off the face of the earth. It'd been risky enough stowing away on his boat. She'd really hoped she wouldn't need to use her backup plan, but she had. And Demetri had played his part wonderfully. She couldn't allow him to screw it up now.

"What—" he started.

She kissed him again. At first it was to shut him up. As his lips softened and he fully participated in the embrace, she let herself enjoy the moment. It had been a long time, if ever, since she'd been kissed so well. For a second she forgot she was wearing only a towel and that two men who wanted to make her disappear stood outside the door. And that moment of memory loss made the man she was kissing potentially more dangerous than the two outside.

Wrenching her lips from his, she whispered in his ear. "They can probably hear everything we say. And do. We're only safe to talk in the shower." Although safe was a relative term when it came to her naked body pressed up against his.

He nodded. However, rather than heading toward the bathroom, he said loud enough for the men outside to clearly hear, "I need to eat before I make love to you again, *glykia mou*. Let's dress and go to dinner. We have all night to celebrate our marriage."

"Good idea. I'm starved." It would buy her some time to figure out how she was going to explain this mess.

Relieved that he didn't demand an immediate explanation for her actions, she grabbed the small satchel that she'd hid in the closet. She tilted her head toward the bathroom, and he nodded an affirmation. Once safely away from everyone, she crumpled onto the floor.

Her attempt to rescue her beloved uncle from an Egyptian prison had so far gotten herself, and an innocent bystander, held at gunpoint and virtual prisoners on this yacht. At least the conditions were a hell of a lot better than her uncle was currently enduring, but it wasn't over yet. She had to convince the gunmen that she and Demetri were wildly in love so they'd leave. Demetri would undoubtedly get rid of her as soon as possible, hopefully at the first island they came across. Then she could make her way to Libya from where she hoped to sneak across the Egyptian border, find her uncle, and bribe the guards to release him. Easy. Not.

None of it was going to happen with her lying on the bathroom floor. She picked herself up and pulled out one of two dresses she'd brought with her, a very skimpy red number that could be crumpled into a ball and still come out looking okay. It probably wasn't the type of dress Demetri Christodoulou's women wore, having only cost her ten euros at a market in Italy. It would have to do.

Through the bathroom door she could hear Demetri talking to someone, demanding to know what was being done about the intruders. He didn't seem satisfied by the answer as several expletives in Greek followed a long silence. A twinge of guilt unsettled her stomach for the position she'd put him in. She turned the water on to brush her teeth and missed the rest of the conversation. She finger combed her hair, touched up her eye makeup, and took a deep breath. Show time.

It was a good thing she took a deep breath in the bathroom because it all whooshed out when she saw Demetri. Greek Gods move over, there was a new deity in town. He hadn't bothered to comb his towel-dried hair, so the ebony curls ran riot, including one that nestled over his forehead, Superman style. His dark eyes and the designer stubble along his jaw emphasized his manliness. He had on a pair of black dress pants and a light blue button-down shirt. The top three buttons were undone, revealing a strong neck and a thick matting of dark hair. His short sleeves stretched tight over his bulging biceps. There was a fluttering sensation in her chest, which was damned annoying. She needed to stay grounded and focused, not aroused and unbalanced.

His dark gaze flared when he saw her in her little red dress. With only string ties around her neck and back holding the front in place, she hadn't worn a bra. Besides, the only one she'd brought still dangled from the lamp next to the sofa. Under his intense stare, her nipples hardened, something that would be clearly visible to him through the thin fabric. To hide from his gaze, she bent and slipped on her sandals. Shame she didn't have her shoe collection at home to choose from. When planning a covert operation, a minimal wardrobe had been the first wise decision. And, it appeared, her last good idea. Then again, she hadn't really expected to play the part of wife to a millionaire Greek hotelier.

It had been sheer luck when she'd been lurking around Athens two weeks ago to discover that Demetri Christodoulou was about to take possession of his new yacht and sail it to Crete. She'd found out all she could about the man, even followed him to Albania so they would both have the stamps on their passports if she needed to prove they knew each other. The fake marriage certificate had been a last-minute decision, one she was glad about now.

"Are you ready?" His deep voice skittered across her taut nerves. The room suddenly seemed to shrink in size. If they were going to convince the armed men that they were truly married, they'd have to share it tonight. Her gaze was drawn to the sofa, which way too short for the 6'2" man who towered over her in her flats. At 5'3" herself, a pair of four-inch heels would barely put a dent in their height difference.

She was about to open the door when his large hand on her arm stopped her. "Wait *glykia mou*, you forgot to put your rings back on," he said. His flawless English held a note of a British accent. She'd lived the last five years in Montreal, Canada, so she had a North American inflection when she spoke her second language. Until she knew where she stood, she'd keep it to herself that she was also fluent in Greek.

He reached into his pocket and pulled out a huge diamond ring and a simple gold band. Taking her hand, he slid both rings onto her finger. Why was he carrying around wedding rings? Her gaze shot to his left hand. Yup, a shiny gold band sat there. Unable to question him without her guards hearing, she was left with only a raised eyebrow to signal her query. A lazy smile crossed his lips at her confusion. She wasn't the only one with a game in play.

Keeping her hand in his, he strode toward the door and wrenched it open. Sure enough, one of the armed men stood right outside.

"You are not invited to dinner," Demetri said to the man.

The guard nodded but followed them down the hall anyway. A table was set up on the rear deck, complete with candles and a flower arrangement with champagne chilling in an ice bath. Her knees wobbled when she saw the table was set for two. The ruse would have been up if his crew had prepared dinner for one.

"I know we'd planned to dine in our room, but I asked the

staff to set up a table out here so we can eat under the stars." He kissed her temple as he helped her into a chair.

"You are so thoughtful, Demetri." She forced a relaxed smile. She'd started this charade; he'd taken it to another level. This man was very good at keeping up a deception. She may yet make it out alive.

They dined quietly, the guard standing close enough to be able to hear should they whisper, but not so close as to loom over them. She hoped he attributed their stilted conversation to his presence and not the fact that she and Demetri were strangers.

Still, her every nerve was on end and any second she expected Demetri to stand up and declare that until an hour ago he'd never laid eyes on her. He must have some ulterior motive for his easy compliance. As she stared at him across the table, he winked. Yes, he was definitely up to something.

She put down her fork, having pushed her dessert around the plate for the past ten minutes. Demetri took her hand in his. "Shall we dance under the moonlight?"

With music playing, they could whisper into each other's ears, and the gunman wouldn't be able to hear them. She nodded and within a minute a crew member brought out a music system and set it on the deck. Demetri pressed play and the rich, seductive voice of Ella Fitzgerald filled the air. He was full of surprises. She'd never have pegged him for a classical jazz lover, although, in her defense, she'd been a bit too busy in the past two hours to think about his musical taste.

He gently pulled her from her chair, walked her over to the middle of the deck, and then tucked her body against his. His lips rested on her temple.

"So, *wife*, would you mind telling me why I'm being held hostage on my own boat with a known enemy of the Egyptian people?" He whispered the words but there was a tone of command in them.

"My uncle is a political prisoner in Egypt. He did nothing wrong except stand up for democracy. My family has been trying to get him released using their government connections with no success. I decided to try a more direct route."

"Are you a terrorist?" His question was immediately followed by a graze of his lips across her forehead to the other temple. It took a moment for her to understand his words, a hesitation she hoped he didn't interpret as guilt.

"Of course not. I have no interest in politics...or religious fanaticism. But I'm also not going to sit around and wait for my uncle to be tortured to death."

"And how exactly did you plan on freeing your uncle?" His hand on her back made a leisurely trip down her spine to her ass, pulling her even closer to him as the song ended. With her head tucked into Demetri's neck, facing away from their audience, she had no idea if he was putting on a show for the gunman or just taking advantage of the moment. Another song began. Ella crooned about wanting someone to watch over her. Rania could do with fewer watchers.

"Stealth, guile, and a shit-load of money," she said. Her breath hitched as his hand wandered up her bare back again, his fingers toying with one of the ties holding the top of her dress in place.

"And where do you expect to get this shit-load of money?" He stopped dancing. The hand at her back anchored her to his muscled form. He released his grip on her hand, and with his fingers under her chin and his thumb along her jaw, forced her gaze to his. To an observer it probably looked like a loving embrace. She felt the force in his touch.

"I have my sources. They don't include you if that's what you're worried about."

"Then why me? Why did you board my boat without permission?"

Should she tell him she'd followed him for two weeks

to make sure he wouldn't hurt her if he found out she was aboard? No. She didn't think Demetri Christodoulou would appreciate being targeted. And if she could get off this boat soon enough, he'd never find out.

"You were in the right place at the right time. Although I guess that interpretation would depend on how you feel about a naked woman invading your shower and machine guns being pointed at your head."

A small smile lifted his lips. "I'll decide that when I see how this plays out."

"I'm sorry I got you into this mess. I'd hoped to hitch a lift to Crete undetected. I heard that your boat was heading south, and I slipped aboard while the crew was loading supplies. I'd intended to hide out in the cabin next to yours until you docked. But when the agents came aboard and started to look for me, I had to improvise. Someone must have ratted me out to the Egyptian authorities. I sensed I was being watched but I wasn't sure. I'm new to covert operations."

"And the Albanian wedding certificate? How did you know I'd been there?"

"I overheard one of your crew say that as soon as you returned from Albania they would be leaving. So I acquired the fake document just in case. I'd hoped I wouldn't need it."

"How did you get my full name and date of birth?"

"It's all on the Internet. Haven't you Googled yourself recently?"

"Do I look like a man who Googles himself?" He ran his thumb over her lips. Damn, he was a convincing lover.

"No, you seem more of a DuckDuckGo guy."

His laugh drowned out the music for a moment then he resumed dancing. "Well, for better or worse, I'm involved now." She wondered if he'd deliberately used the marital term. Before she could ask, he continued. "But if I find you've lied to me or try to scam me for money, I won't hesitate in handing you over personally to the Egyptian government."

"What about the rings? Is there a woman somewhere who's going to scratch my eyes out for pretending to be your wife?"

"I'd put my money on you if it came to a fight." He hadn't answered her question. Even with all her spying she hadn't been able to discover anything about his personal life, which had played in nicely to the Egyptians not knowing if he was married or not. But obviously he had someone in his life to have wedding rings on board. The question was who? And would they understand her predicament?

The song ended and they both stood, not even a hair's breadth between them, staring into the other's eyes. He nodded and a crew member who had been hovering out of sight rushed forward and shut off the music.

Demetri cleared his throat and then said loudly enough for their guard to hear, "It's bedtime, wife. You promised me a night full of love."

Chapter Two

Rania swallowed. Is this where she paid the piper? She loved her uncle as much as her own father. Uncle Fouad had supported her and encouraged her to get a degree and was going to train her to be his successor. Her father still held the antiquated idea that a woman's place was at home, caring for her children. Not that she had anything against family or children. Her three sisters had found great happiness in their marriages. Rania wanted more. What more she didn't exactly know. It sure as hell wasn't the thrill of getting a huge discount on a bulk order of diapers.

Demetri took her hand and led her through the maze of passages back to the main stateroom. In their absence it had been tidied and the bed remade, the corners of both sides turned down. She'd felt bad about trashing the immaculate room earlier, but it had helped to cement the passionate romance theme. The gunman quickly searched the area, including checking in the adjoining bathroom. Did he think she had a spare husband in there? Apparently satisfied that she couldn't escape, he retreated to the doorway.

"I or my colleague will be in the hallway all night. Do not lock the door or we will be forced to shoot it open. Enjoy your night." An evil sneer accompanied his words.

Demetri clenched his fists as though about to strike the man. Rania put her hand on her fake husband's face, trying to soothe his anger. She had really done a number on him. When his eyes met hers, she let him see her terror. It seemed to spark his protector instinct, and he pulled her against him, sheltering her with his body.

What would it have been like if they'd have met under other circumstances? Would this wild chemistry between them even exist? Or was it a product of danger and the forced proximity of their mock marriage?

Whatever the reason for the attraction, she wasn't going to give in to it and have sex with a stranger. Except to the man outside, it had to seem that Demetri was her husband and they were on their honeymoon.

Reluctantly, she pulled out of his arms and grabbed the pad of paper and pen she'd seen earlier in the bedside cabinet and wrote a quick note.

We have to pretend to have sex.

Why pretend? Demetri wrote back.

Because I don't have sex with strangers.

We're married. You have the fake paperwork to prove it.

He started to unbutton his shirt, and she threw the paper on the bed and dived into the bathroom. Thankfully, her satchel was still in there and she quickly pulled on a pair of shorts and a tank top. Not quite the seductive lingerie she imagined Demetri's bedmates usually wore. *I'm not trying to seduce the guy. Keep your head, girl. You can't afford to screw this up now.*

Demetri sat in the bed, his chest bare, the sheet pooled at his waist. Oh God, what if he's naked? *Bam*, composure incinerated. She just managed to stop from licking her lips.

Forcing her eyes from his muscled torso, her gaze flickered to the sofa but he shook his head when she glanced back at him. He was right. If for some reason one of their guards checked on them in the night, her sleeping on the sofa would be a death-knell to their charade. She'd be hauled off to join her uncle in prison, and who knew what they'd do to Demetri for lying to them.

She climbed onto the other side of the bed and bounced on the mattress.

He grabbed the notepaper she'd left and quickly wrote, *What are you doing?* Due to her bouncing, his writing was shaky and hard to read.

I'm trying to get the bed to creak like we're making love, she wrote back.

If this bed creaks during sex, simulated or not, I will turn this boat around right now and take it back to the builder.

Okay, but we need to make the guy outside believe we're married.

"G*lykia mou,* you are so beautiful, your breasts are so full and tasty." She jumped at Demetri's loud voice. She glared at him. He was going to ruin the whole thing by his cheesy acting.

She grabbed the notepaper and quickly scribbled. *Stop it. That sounds ridiculous. No one says those things during sex. Be natural!*

"*Habibi,* yes, yes! Right there, that's the spot," she said, ending on a low moan, loud enough for their audience.

Demetri grabbed the paper and pen. *Now you're not natural. I don't need directions. I KNOW how to make love to a woman.* The word KNOW was double underlined.

Rania giggled. Demetri glared back at her then a grin lifted his lips. She sucked in a breath. Damn, he was gorgeous when he smiled.

"Already? You said you could last a little longer this

time?" she said loudly.

One more comment like that and I will show you exactly how long I can last.

"Oh, *habibi*, you're so wonderful. I've never known loving like yours."

"That's because we're in love," he replied. "I still remember the day I first saw you—"

She elbowed him in the ribs to shut him up.

"I'm tired now and need to sleep. It's been a rather eventful day." She finished with a loud, fake yawn.

"You promised me a whole night of non-stop sex. That was just the warm-up."

She punched him in the arm. He caught her hand and kissed his rings on her finger.

"Pace yourself. We have the rest of our lives." Her voice was a little breathless as he held her gaze. His eyes promised what he would do to her if they were truly married.

Was the guy outside even still there?

"All right, *glykia mou*. I'll let you get your sleep. You'll need to be well rested for tomorrow."

If she thought he'd turn over and sleep on his side of the bed, she was sadly mistaken. He pulled her against him, anchoring her to his firm body with an iron arm. There was no way she'd be able to sleep now.

"Relax, Rania. I won't let anything bad happen to you," he whispered. He hadn't called her by name before, and it sent a flutter along her nerve endings. With her head on his chest, she felt as much as heard the words. For the first time in weeks, a sense of security wrapped around her. How long would it last? And when would the rightful wearer of his ring come to claim it?

• • •

Demetri woke with Rania lying practically on top of him. Her head was in the middle of his chest, her arm across his abdomen, her hand on his waist, a leg over both of his. And her hair was everywhere—on the pillow, across his stomach, down her back. A strand even lay across her face, rising and falling in concert with her breathing. He usually liked long hair on women, but Rania's chestnut waves had hidden her torso from view yesterday when she'd joined him in the shower, so he was a little resentful.

He inhaled deeply of her cinnamon and nutmeg scent, mixed with an earthy musk and a hint of jasmine undertones. It was exotic and sensual and fit her perfectly. Christina smelled of flowers and sunshine. A stab of guilt sliced through him as he thought of his girlfriend. He'd made no commitment to her; in fact, their relationship was very casual. He'd visited her each time he returned to Gavdos, but they didn't keep in touch between trips. Yet it seemed wrong to be thinking of her when he was lying in bed with another woman, especially a woman as tempting as Rania.

His hand wandered down her back, repeating the journey it had made last night when they'd danced. He'd come mighty close to losing it then. His cock stirred to life even remembering her in that red dress. If she were really his wife, he would forbid her to wear it outside of their home. No other man would ogle his woman. His breath hitched at the erotic images that flooded his mind—visions of releasing the ties that had held it to her chest, watching the soft fabric fall to her waist…

Rania stirred. Her hand slid from his side, across his lower abdomen before settling again on his upper thigh. He had to get out of here now before the guard outside the door heard the real noises of lovemaking, heard Rania scream Demetri's name as he rocked her world from under her. He'd take her to heights she didn't even know existed. Then next time there'd be no fake moans and called-out instructions.

Next time? What the hell am I thinking?

He had to get out of bed. Now. Get these men off his boat, drop Rania at the first island they came across, and propose to Christina. Except his arm automatically tightened around the woman next to him. The small part of the male genetic code, the desire to be a woman's knight in shining armor, rejected that plan. Rania needed him. He needed a wife to buy the land on Gavdos for his resort. Marriage to Rania held two advantages over an attachment to Christina.

First, he could set a time limit on their relationship. A year would probably suffice. They'd both get what they wanted and then go their separate ways. He'd get his land; she'd get his protection as she tried to free her uncle. Being shackled to one woman for the rest of his life had been a price he'd been willing to pay to get the property. Now he didn't have to. Christina was far too nice a girl to divorce. Although he didn't love her, he was fond of her. A divorce would break her heart; he couldn't do that to her. Rania would probably take divorce in stride. She'd be glad to get her freedom back.

Second, he could explore the passion that simmered between them. So far he'd only shared a few chaste kisses with Christina. She came from a very strict family, and he hadn't wanted to take her virginity before the wedding night. That and the fact that nothing she'd said, or done, or any looks she'd given him, had set his skin on fire. Unlike Rania. All she had to do was touch his hand and he wanted to fling her over his shoulder, take her somewhere private, and ravage her until they both were exhausted. He figured a year would probably be sufficient to get the lust out of his system as well. Yes, Rania would make a great temporary wife.

That decided, he eased out from under her. The soft sound of protest that escaped her lips nearly had him climbing back into bed. If they were really married, he wouldn't get out of bed at all today. But they weren't. And he had plans to set in motion.

He found the paper they'd used last night to write notes to each other. He ripped off the top sheets and a few more underneath. He read her comments again and smiled. That was another thing Rania brought to the bedroom—laughter. Passion and laughter, it was an enticing combination. He carefully hid the notes. He'd get rid of them later so the gunmen couldn't find evidence of their fraud.

It was almost a disappointment when Rania didn't invade his shower again. And when he strolled through the bedroom with a towel around his hips, she didn't even stir. He stood for a minute and watched her sleep, her chest rising and falling with each breath. She whispered his name and he froze. For some unknown reason, his heart rate accelerated. Maybe it was being caught doing something he shouldn't, although all he was doing was watching a woman sleep in his own bed. Must be the wicked thoughts running through his mind at the same time accounting for the guilt. She rolled over and continued sleeping.

He dressed quickly—before his body could convince his mind to climb back into bed and wake her the way a husband should wake his wife. Their not-so-friendly Egyptian agent was waiting outside the stateroom door; the second one, not the one who had been there when they'd gone to bed. At least Demetri wasn't faced with the smirk on the other man's face from Rania's lame sex talk.

"My wife is still sleeping. Wake her, or do anything to her, and you won't see out the day. That I promise," Demetri told him. He'd send one of his crew down to make sure the man didn't enter their room.

The guard nodded and resumed staring at the door.

Demetri made his way to the bridge to speak with the captain. He wasn't surprised to find the other gunman there.

Ignoring the Egyptian intruder, the captain greeted Demetri with a smile. They spoke in Greek. If the gunman understood or not, he didn't say anything. Unfortunately, the Coast Guard and Navy in the area were dealing with two boatloads of illegal immigrants, one of which had capsized. They'd advised Demetri's captain to make for the nearest port where the land-based authorities would deal with their unwelcome guests.

Demetri glanced over at the gunman who eyed him steadily. If they were going to be killed, it would have happened by now, probably while they slept. And having them on board meant Rania would be forced to pretend to be his wife. He had to admit, he enjoyed that.

"Keep on the route we discussed. Alert the authorities in Kissamos that two foreign nationals will be disembarking. Then my wife and I will head on to Gavdos as planned," Demetri said to the captain. That would give him one more day to play husband, and then one day to convince Rania to make the arrangement semi-permanent. He smiled and went to find his breakfast.

· · ·

Rania woke with a start. Something was missing. She could hear the boat's engines and the gentle sound of the waves slapping the hull. They were still moving, and Demetri was gone. His side of the bed was cold so it wasn't a recent departure.

She sat up and pushed her hair out of her face. Normally she braided it before she went to sleep but she'd forgotten last night. Last night. A smile crept over her face. Despite the gunmen and the threat of death, and worrying about her hastily knit web of lies unraveling, she'd had fun. Demetri was a charming companion. In different circumstances, one she'd like to spend more time with.

Time was one thing she didn't have. Each day her uncle spent in prison the risk of his death grew greater. If he was still alive. The last contact they'd had with him had been two months ago, and the only thing he was guilty of was saying that all Egyptians, no matter their religion or political affiliation, deserved for their voices to be heard, which was why she'd embarked on this ridiculous mission. At least she was doing something and not sitting around waiting for someone else to take action.

Speaking of action, she'd better get out of bed and find Demetri. She glanced at the clock; it was barely eight. What time had he risen? And why hadn't he woken her? They probably could have put on another performance for their audience. Her body tingled in places it shouldn't. Maybe it wasn't such a smart idea to pretend to have sex with Demetri. Made her want the real thing too much.

She searched for the notepad they'd used last night to communicate. It wasn't under her pillow where she'd put it. A cold shiver raced down her spine. Had Demetri taken it to show the gunmen? Used it to bargain for his own safety and that of his crew? After all, what did she really know about him? For a guy to be so successful at thirty, he was probably used to all sorts of shady dealings. According to a sketchy Wikipedia entry, he'd built his resort empire from nothing. She was only three years younger, came from money, and the only achievement she could claim was a shoe collection that was the envy of her sisters.

She shook her head. Demetri may be many things, yet he'd immediately come to her aid, without explanation, yesterday. And he'd promised he wouldn't let anything bad happen to her. Most importantly, he'd called her Rania, not *glykia mou*, my sweet, which he probably called his grandmother's cat. It was like her calling him *habibi*, my dear; it meant nothing. When she fell in love, she'd call her man *azizy*, my darling, or *hobi,* my love, something with meaning. That, too, was a long way off.

In the meantime, she needed to get dressed and find her fake husband. She had a quick shower. As she dried herself she decided not to analyze the sense of loss she felt. She hadn't wanted Demetri to join her; it would have complicated things too much. And the very last thing she needed right now was another complication, no matter how much her body wanted one.

What to wear? Shorts and a T-shirt? How would Demetri's real wife dress? Probably not the five-dollar T-shirt announcing a star is born. Or the eight-dollar shorts with heart-shaped pockets. They had been part of her blend-in-as-a-tourist wardrobe. She had a choice between her swimsuit and the one other dress she'd brought. She hung the dress up to wear to dinner tonight, in case they still had their company, and put on her white bikini and blue knit cover-up. Not her usual breakfast attire, but she was, after all, on a boat in the middle of the Mediterranean Sea. It had to be appropriate.

She opened the door and by the expression on the gunman's face, she might have made a major mistake. Donning her haughtiest expression, she breezed past him and headed for the upper deck. She could smell bacon and toast, and suddenly she was ravenous.

"Good morning, sleepyhead. Did I exhaust you so much last night?" Demetri's deep voice behind her made her jump, which she quickly disguised by throwing herself into his arms.

Forget breakfast. He looked good enough to eat. White shorts emphasized his long legs and a navy T-shirt hugged his broad shoulders, muscled chest, and massive biceps. All she needed was a jar of honey and… This line of thought was going to end in disaster. She gave him a quick kiss on the lips before leaning back on his arm, which anchored her lower body to his.

"There you are, *habibi*. I was lonely when I woke. Where did you get to?" As innocent as her question was, she hoped his reply was more meaningful.

"I was making arrangements to get rid of our unwelcome audience. Unfortunately, they're with us for another twenty-four hours. So we must be on our best behavior and confine our amorous activities to our stateroom."

She searched his eyes. Twenty-four hours? Was he serious? Where was the Greek Navy or Coast Guard? Or why hadn't they pulled into the nearest port? Had Demetri made a deal with the *friends of the Egyptian government* to deliver her straight to Egypt? When Uncle Fouad had first been arrested, she'd gotten the international media interested in his case, which had caused a lot of embarrassment for the current regime. There was probably a tidy little sum on her head if it had been worthwhile for these two to illegally board Demetri's boat. Her uncle wasn't the richest man in Egypt, but pretty close. And with him already in custody, his fortune would probably be forfeited to the government if they held his heiress, too.

Demetri must have read her mind, because he put one hand on her face, cupping it. His thumb swept under her eye as though removing a tear. "Don't worry, *glykia mou*. I promised to keep you safe, and I never go back on a promise. Now, come have some breakfast. I can't have you fainting on me from lack of food."

Pasting on a saucy smile for their audience, she kissed his palm and then sauntered over to the table, laid out as it had been last night, minus the champagne. He took the opposite chair, his hot gaze roving over her body.

"If I'd known we were to have company on this cruise, I'd have insisted you pack more clothes," Demetri said.

Rania glanced down then back up at Demetri. There was raw passion in his eyes. She'd worn either severe business suits or boring, respectable dresses for the past five years. None of the previous men in her life had gazed at her that way. It was more than lust. It was possession. She wasn't quite sure how to take it.

In fact her last boyfriend had been more impressed with her bank account and her prospective inheritance than her rack and booty. He'd definitely never made the back of her thighs tingle and her breasts physically ache to be touched. Demetri managed it with just a look. And his smile said he knew exactly what he was doing to her.

"I'm starved," she said, trying to get her breathing under control.

Demetri waved his hand, and immediately two crew members appeared with a selection of breakfast items.

"So, what did your family say about our hasty marriage?" Demetri asked as she sipped her orange juice. She coughed as it went down the wrong way. It was rather awkward to find out things a normal married couple would already know, without their audience realizing that they were strangers.

"My parents were a bit surprised, but then, I'm known in my family for doing outrageous things. They can't wait to meet you. My father may be able to take a vacation from his position at the British Museum and come to Greece in a couple of months. My three sisters all think I'm crazy anyway. They plan to hold a big party for us when we eventually make it to Montreal. What about your family?"

"I haven't told them yet," Demetri said with a lazy grin.

She relaxed a bit. Obviously, he planned to get her off his boat before they got anywhere near his family.

"Don't be surprised if they insist on having another ceremony once they find out," he added.

Her gaze shot to his. What was he saying?

"Yes, *glykia mou*, we will be getting married again once we arrive at Gavdos."

Chapter Three

Demetri glanced over at Rania sunbathing next to the lap pool. She'd dispensed with the cover-up and lay in full glory in her tiny white bikini. He'd seen a lot of beautiful sights cruising around the Greek islands. But Rania on his deck was the most breathtaking and the most distracting. He'd been trying to work on the plans for the Gavdos resort for almost half an hour now and still couldn't concentrate.

He was supposed to be on vacation, anyway. He shut down his laptop and strolled over to Rania. "Careful you don't burn, *glykia mou*. At sea the sun is stronger than you think. I'd better put more sunscreen on you." He grabbed the bottle of lotion next to her and squeezed a generous amount into his hands. As he rubbed them together he met her gaze. She swallowed, then glared at him. With their audience, she couldn't really protest her *husband* touching her. She flipped over onto her stomach. Well, he'd always enjoyed a challenge.

"I… Oh God," she ended with a groan as he swept one hand up her leg, his fingers lingering over her inner thigh, stroking toward her center. His index finger deliberately grazed the fabric of her bathing suit between her legs, eliciting a loud moan.

"That sounds more natural," he leaned in and whispered in her ear before rubbing cream up her other leg. He slid a finger under the edge of her bikini bottom this time, and she shuddered. He had to shift his own body as it responded to touching her. Maybe this wasn't such a good idea. But now that he'd started…

He undid the ties at her back and nape. Her hair was piled on top of her head, exposing her long, graceful neck. After kissing her under her right ear, inhaling her heady scent, he creamed up her arms and over her shoulder muscles, which were unusually tense. After finishing her back, he hauled in a deep breath and then slid his hands to her sides, lingering on the soft swell of her breasts.

Rania, took a deep breath which lifted her body higher, allowing his fingers another centimeter of access. Her whole body quivered under his touch.

"Turn over and let me do your front," he said, although he'd probably end up doing more than applying sunscreen.

"Demetri, we have an audience," she reminded him, her voice low and husky.

He glanced over at the two Egyptian agents who both appeared as hot and bothered as he was feeling. One of them shifted where he was sitting. As much as Demetri was personally enjoying tormenting Rania, he wasn't about to share the fun with the other men.

"You're right. We'll continue this when we're alone." He pulled off his T-shirt and dived into the pool, hoping the cool water would relieve the pressure in his swim trunks. He swam against the artificial current until his arms and legs burned.

When he pulled himself out of the water, both guards were gone, and Rania stood by the railing, staring out to sea.

He should leave her alone, but couldn't. She drew him to

her like a magnet. Not bothering to towel off, he put his arms around her. The heat off her body could have created steam from the water on his. He drifted kisses from her shoulder to under her ear. She tilted her head to allow him greater access.

"This was such a bad idea," she whispered.

"What was?"

Her head lolled back onto his shoulder. His hands crept up her torso until they rested just under her full breasts. His thumbs swept over her nipples, and they instantly pebbled under his touch. Already his body had hardened again. His erection strained against his swim trunks, pushing into her back.

"Stowing away aboard your boat, pretending to be married to you." She moaned again as his thumbs circled her nipples through the thin fabric of her bikini top. Before he could do it again, she swiveled, her arms going around his waist, her cheek against his heart.

"I don't know. It seems to be working. Where have the agents gone?"

"Probably to have a cold shower. You're a very convincing husband." He forced his hands to stay still on her back, not rove up and down as they wanted, not pull her closer to him until every one of her curves was molded into him. After all, she wasn't his wife, wasn't even his girlfriend. She was a woman in trouble. He shouldn't add to her distress, no matter how incredible it felt. Then again, she'd started it; he was only playing along.

"You haven't seen anything yet," he said.

"Please, Demetri. I can't take much more of this."

Twenty-four hours ago she'd barged into his shower and begged him to help her. Twenty-four hours ago he'd been contemplating marriage to Christina. Twenty-four hours ago he'd been sane.

"It would be amazing. I'd make sure of that."

"I don't doubt it, but I have to rescue my uncle not have a torrid affair with you."

Out of the corner of his eye he caught sight of one of the Egyptian agents returning to the deck. He put a thumb under Rania's jaw and raised her face to his.

"This was part of your plan," he said.

She laughed, a pure, blissful sound that ruffled the hair on his chest. "If you haven't worked it out yet, *habibi*, I'm not so good with actual plans. I come up with some half-assed idea and then jump in with both feet and try to figure out what to do as I fall."

"Let me catch you this time." He kissed her long and hard until she melted against him. One of her arms slid up his body, around his neck, and into his hair. Before he ripped the bikini from her body and took her right there on the deck, he released her. They both sucked in lungfuls of air, and he forced his eyes from her heaving chest.

One of the Egyptian agents approached. "Tell your captain to slow down, Mr. Christodoulou. Our boat will come alongside and we will get off. However, I warn you to keep your wife away from Egypt. If she tries to free her uncle, it will not be good for her. Or you."

Rania began to argue in Arabic. As the man reached for his gun, Demetri pulled her to his side. She was going to get herself killed if he didn't look after her. "Easy, *glykia mou*; let's get rid of them so we can enjoy the rest of our honeymoon."

He led her over to the intercom on the wall, ordering the captain to halt the yacht. As the engines powered down, the high-pitched whine of a motorboat filled the air. The second Egyptian agent appeared and hooked a rope ladder over onto the railing and threw the rest of it over the side of the boat. Five minutes later, they were both gone, the ladder flapping in the breeze as the motorboat with its human cargo sped toward a larger ship barely visible on the horizon.

Rania turned and opened her mouth. Before she could say anything he swept her into his arms and whispered into her ear. "I suggest we keep up the pretense until I can get a security specialist to check the boat for microphones and hidden cameras."

"Really?" Her warm breath caressed his neck, and he repressed a shiver of delight.

"It's what I would do in their position. While we were up here on deck, I'm sure they were in our stateroom. They may be gone, but I bet they're still watching and listening, probably hoping to find out what you plan to do next." She slumped against him, defeated. "We'll figure out something. I promise," he said.

She raised her gorgeous face, her almond-colored eyes full of questions. "You're the best husband I've ever had." She laughed and an odd warmth invaded his chest. Too much sun, not enough food.

"We're a couple hours from Milos. Why don't we stop and have dinner at one of the restaurants there." His suggestion was greeted with a smile, and his chest got tighter. Definitely too much sun.

• • •

Rania slipped into the last dress she'd brought with her, a black floaty creation she hoped would be suitable for the restaurant where Demetri had reserved a table. She'd spent ten minutes in the shower, scrubbing off the sunscreen, in a vain attempt to erase the feel of his hands on her body. He could reduce her to a quivering mess with only a touch. She didn't appreciate the power he had over her body. She had to make sure her head stayed in command. *There's a first time for everything.* Then the bathroom door clicked open, and Demetri walked in. Any thought she had about being in control evaporated in the heat of his gaze. He was still bare-chested and his swim trunks sat low on his hips. To stop from licking her lips, she tried to concentrate on applying her lipstick.

"If you're done with the shower—"

She grabbed her small makeup bag and fled the bathroom, her shoulder brushing his naked chest as she passed. Damn the man, but he was tempting.

She'd managed to get her eyeliner almost even when Demetri opened the door. His hair was still damp, a riot of curls, a white towel wrapped around his hips. A girl had to know her limits.

"I'll wait for you on deck," she said, her voice a little too breathless for her liking. She grabbed her one pair of heeled shoes and escaped the cabin. Demetri's laugh followed her down the hallway like a challenge. The competitor in her wanted to march right back in there and turn him into a quivering heap of gelatinous mass. The pragmatist told her this was one battle she couldn't win.

As she waited in the lounge, her mind replayed Demetri's statements from earlier in the day. Had his words about getting married "again" on Gavdos been simply for their audience? Was he really going to help find and free her uncle?

When she'd returned to their cabin, she'd had a quick glance around for listening devices or hidden cameras. Everything had appeared in order, yet she still felt on edge. And Demetri was right. They probably were being watched, which meant she couldn't stay in Milos tonight. If she didn't return to the boat, the Egyptians would know in minutes and probably pick her up within hours.

And she still hadn't found the paper where she'd written notes to Demetri that first night. First night, it was last night. Odd how it seemed she'd known him so much longer. Maybe it was the two weeks she'd trailed him before she'd set foot on his boat. She'd been impressed with the way he treated everyone from hotel bellboys to government officials. And when he'd stopped to help an old lady in Albania pick up her groceries after she'd been knocked over by a jerk on a bike, Rania knew he was a good guy. He'd even slipped the old lady some money to make up for her lost produce, which had been squished by passing cars. A man that thoughtful wouldn't rape her and toss her overboard.

But it didn't mean she wanted to keep playing his wife for long. Tonight at the restaurant, hopefully away from any listening ears, she'd convince him to stop in Crete. There they could have the boat cleared of cameras and bugs, then she could slip ashore someplace and disappear, maybe make her way to Turkey and eventually through to Jordan and find someone willing to slip into Egypt for her and bribe the right people for her uncle's freedom. It was as good a plan as she could come up with at the moment. So why did she still feel so deflated?

Demetri appeared wearing a tailor-made suit. The dark fabric emphasized his broad shoulders and expanse of chest. His light-blue shirt had the top two buttons undone at his neck. This time Rania did lick her lips. She'd always been a sucker for a man in a well-fitted suit.

The boat bumped lightly against the dock, and Demetri's arms came around her, preventing her from falling back onto the sofa where she'd been sitting.

"I may have to give up my day job. Rescuing you is becoming a full-time occupation," he said, steering her out to the gangplank.

"I'm not helpless."

"I never said you were, but we could all use a little assistance now and then. For example, there's something you could help me with."

"What's that?"

He put a finger on her lips. "I'll tell you after dinner. It's a short walk to the restaurant, but I could call a taxi to take us if you prefer."

"No, I could use the exercise." What she hadn't counted on, however, was the continual pitch of the land. In two short days her legs had become used to the roll of the boat beneath her. Demetri's solid arm around her waist kept her somewhat steady. "They probably won't serve me a drink thinking I'm intoxicated already."

"Give it a few minutes. Your legs will adjust."

"How come you don't have a problem?"

"Maybe I do. Maybe you're the one holding me up."

She laughed and he tightened his arm around her. The restaurant owner greeted Demetri like a long-lost son before ushering them to a secluded table at the edge of the patio where their table did have a magnificent view. They looked out onto the harbor and the boats bobbing gently in the water. Rania could easily pick out Demetri's boat, the most magnificent one there. Across the water, the hill was populated with white-washed homes, their brightly painted doors a pop of color in the fading sun. Fairy lights in the pergola above and candles on the table provided soft light in the fast-approaching dusk. It was the ultimate romantic setting.

"Giorgio opened specially for us," Demetri said. "With the tourist season closing down he's usually only open four nights a week."

"I hope we haven't inconvenienced him. I don't mind where we eat." The proprietor arrived with a bottle of wine. He looked old enough to be her grandfather's grandfather.

"He would never speak to me again if I was nearby and went somewhere else, would you, Giorgio?" Demetri repeated the question in Greek.

Giorgio laughed and poured the wine, all the while complimenting Demetri on his beautiful woman. She caught him glancing at their rings. She'd considered not putting them back on after her shower. However, if there were cameras on board the boat, she figured she'd better be cautious. It had nothing whatsoever to do with the fact that her chest burned a little when she thought about handing them back to Demetri, probably tomorrow when they said goodbye. She took a long swig of her wine to ease the lump in her throat.

"You've captivated another man, *glykia mou*," Demetri said when Giorgio eventually wandered away. He hadn't offered them menus or asked what they wanted to eat. He'd simply promised something tasty. Speaking of tasty…

"We're alone now. You can stop pretending."

Instead, Demetri raised her hand to his lips and kissed the rings she'd been thinking about. "What would you say if I told you I wanted to turn pretense into reality?"

She pulled her hand out of his grasp. It was hard enough to concentrate with his body so close. When he was touching her, it was nearly impossible. "What do you mean?"

"I mean, I want you to be my wife. For real."

• • •

Rania reached again for her wine and drained half the glass.

"You're not married already are you?" he asked.

"Of course not, but just because I pretended to be married to you doesn't mean I want to make it real."

"You already have. The Egyptian government believes we're married. Giorgio is undoubtedly on the phone this minute calling everyone on my birth island of Gavdos to announce the news. By the time we dock the day after tomorrow, there won't be a single person who knows me who hasn't heard I'm married. It's too late to go back now. You started this game. I'm taking it to the next level."

"You could explain to Giorgio."

"Ah, but I don't want to. Being married to you suits me.

For now. However, that fake Albanian marriage certificate won't pass muster with my mother and grandmother. They'll insist on seeing proof of our marriage for themselves, which will require a real wedding on Gavdos."

"Why? I am sorry if I've put you in a difficult position. I could explain to your family. Tell them what a hero you are. I'm sure they'd understand."

He hadn't seen such panic in her eyes when they were facing two assault rifles in the hands of hostile government agents. For a second he considered letting her off the hook, then she leaned forward and put her hand on his arm and a bolt of desire raced through him.

"I need to marry for business reasons. You're as good as any other woman."

"As good as any other woman?" She jumped from her chair and paced, muttering in Arabic under her breath. She was clearly trying to calm down in order to dissuade him with a rational argument. "Demetri, surely you want to marry a woman you love. Or at least one who loves you? You had rings on board. You must have had someone in mind."

"I did, but you will suffice."

She gave up her attempt at being rational. Her eyes blazed with fury, her hands fisted on her hips. Her anger, her passion, only added to her beauty. "I will suffice? I suffice for no man!"

"Sit down, Rania." He waited until she sat, still quivering with rage. God, she was magnificent. "I'm sorry if I've offended you. Marriage to you has two major advantages over an alliance with another woman."

"Oh, how wonderful. Tell me, Demetri, in what *two* ways am I better than any other woman you know?"

Audacity had a new definition—Rania. He probably wouldn't have to deal with a lot of tears where she was concerned. Make that three positives, although she probably wouldn't appreciate that point so he'd keep it to himself. "First, we have a mutual short-term need. You need the protection of my name while you try to get your uncle out of prison. I need to be married to secure a property I wish to purchase. Once those things are accomplished, we can go our separate ways, no harm no foul. As this isn't a love match, neither of us will be heartbroken when we divorce."

She tilted her head to one side as though considering his words. "And the second reason?"

He reached for her hand and pulled her onto his lap. He kissed her until her hand went from pushing against his chest to sliding around to the back of his head and threading her fingers through his hair. They were both helpless in resisting the attraction between them. He released her lips and buried his face in her hair. "Secondly, we can explore this passion between us in marital-sanctified copulation."

Rania pulled back to stare at his face. Her eyes were narrowed but the glare was ruined by the banked desire evidenced by the heightened flecks of gold in her amber eyes. "Marital-sanctified copulation? Is that your way of talking dirty? Because you aren't going to convince me with those words, Demetri."

He laughed. She did that to him. Made him laugh. Made him think of things other than business. Mostly at this point about how much he wanted to get her in bed. Still, it wasn't business.

"Let me try logic, then. Do you have any legitimate reason why you can't marry me? Would your parents object to me?" Because as much as he wanted her, he wouldn't cause a rift in her family, not like the one in his.

"My parents wouldn't object to my marriage, as long as my husband loves me and is honorable." She raised an eyebrow.

"I am honorable, and if we both agree that love isn't an issue, then I don't see the problem. And you know I can fake it when called upon to do so."

The shuffling sound of Giorgio approaching with their meal spurred Demetri to action. He kissed Rania again until he sensed Giorgio's presence by their table, which was damn hard when most of his senses were overwhelmed with Rania's taste, smell, and the feel of her skin under his hand. He had to convince her to marry him.

Giorgio placed plates of fish before them. So fresh, the fish had probably been swimming in the sea half an hour ago. The restaurant owner lingered at their table until Rania invited him to join them. Whether it was genuine friendliness on her part or she was hoping to keep Demetri in check, he didn't know or particularly care. He had an ace up his sleeve he wasn't averse to playing.

The meal was pleasant. Giorgio tried his best to converse in English; Demetri translated when necessary. Rania was charming and amusing, telling stories of her travels throughout Europe, which invariably started with her getting on the wrong train and ending up somewhere entirely different from where she'd planned to go. Then she'd have the most amazing time and not bother to go to her original destination. By the time they'd finished dessert, if Demetri didn't convince Rania to marry him, he was sure Giorgio would try, despite the fact he already had a wife of sixty years.

"Giorgio, Rania loves to dance. Would you mind playing for us?"

While Giorgio ran off to get his bouzouki, Rania glared.

"What are you doing?"

"I want to dance with my wife."

Before she could reply, Giorgio returned and began to play a haunting melody. Demetri led Rania over to a corner of the restaurant where the tables had been pushed back forming an impromptu dance floor. Putting both her arms around his neck he pulled her flush against his body. His lips rested against the top of her ear, and he gave it a little lick, feeling a shiver course through her whole body.

"Marry me," he whispered.

"No."

"If you don't agree, I'll show the notes we wrote last night to the Egyptian authorities and hand you over personally."

She stopped moving and pulled back as much as he would allow.

"You wouldn't dare." Her eyes searched his in the dim light as if trying to gauge his seriousness.

"Don't underestimate me. When I want something, I get it. At the moment I want a wife, and I want you."

"You are a bastard." She said something else, in Arabic, which he was pretty sure he didn't want translated.

He pulled her against him and whispered into her ear, "Yes, *glykia mou*. But for better or worse, in sickness or in health, I'm your bastard."

Chapter Four

Rania slammed the stateroom door and then the bathroom one for added emphasis. She didn't give a damn if the Egyptian agents returned and carted her off to Cairo. At the moment, it seemed the better option than marriage to Demetri. He could put what spin on it he wanted. He'd blackmailed her. She should call his bluff.

Except the tiny part of her brain not consumed with rage reasoned that this "marriage" could get her what she wanted as well. Demetri was a powerful man in this part of the world. Not only his wealth, but his connections were reputed to be vast. As his wife, she could leverage them to get her uncle free. It was clear the Christodoulou name had kept the Egyptian military from taking her. If she'd been aboard any other boat, she'd be in Cairo or Alexandria right now.

Demetri could buy his land and then she could return to Canada with her uncle. And her husband could rot in hell for all she cared. For Uncle Fouad she'd do it. But if Demetri expected a docile, obedient wife, he'd be sadly disappointed.

A couple of minutes later, the stateroom door clicked

open then shut again. Demetri had stayed behind at Giorgio's to make a few calls away from any listening ears on the boat. She'd stormed off, not wanting to hear him gloat about securing a wife so his precious real estate transaction could go through. She'd called her eldest sister to get the necessary papers sent over so they could obtain a marriage license. Rather than say she was getting married, she told her family she'd lost her passport and needed to get a replacement. Knowing her scatterbrained tendencies they wouldn't question her further. Hopefully, she could be married and divorced before they ever got wind of Demetri and his nefarious plan.

When she stepped into the bedroom a few minutes later, Demetri sat in the bed reading, the sheet pooled at his waist, his chest bare. Tempting. Too bad she was still furious.

"A smart man would know when his wife was angry and go sleep somewhere else."

"I didn't get married to sleep alone. Get in bed, Rania. By tomorrow you'll see I'm right."

She put her hand on the door handle intending to find another bed—a Demetri-free bed—to sleep in.

"Don't bother." His deep voice stopped her before she could open the door. "I'll find you and crawl in beside you. This is the largest bed on the boat. At least here you can have some space apart from me, if you insist. Another bed might not be so accommodating."

Was it another bluff? He appeared serious, and the thought of being curled up against him was too much. She stomped over to the bed and crawled in. "You really are a bastard."

"We've already established that. Go to sleep, Rania. It will all look better in the morning."

In the morning it did look better, because she woke up lying on top of Demetri. And from the death grip her hand had on his pajama bottoms, even if he'd tried to move her, she wouldn't have budged. She raised her head and saw the laughter in his eyes.

"Do you always sleep this way?" he asked. "Because I'm thinking all we need is a single bed in our house."

She went to roll off him but his arms held her where she was. She wriggled a bit until she realized it wasn't a bunched up sheet between them. His erection pressed into her stomach.

"I…no. Usually I like my space. Maybe I was cold in the night. You probably stole all the blankets, and I was trying to get them and got stuck."

"Or maybe when you go to sleep and your brain lets go, your body feels free to seek out what it really wants—me."

"Whatever." She pushed off him and sat up, tossing her braid over her shoulder. "Are we stopping in Crete today? I need to freshen up my wardrobe."

"I don't know. I quite enjoy what you're wearing."

She glanced down. Her nipples were clearly visible through the white tank top, and she'd forgotten to put on her shorts last night so was wearing a skimpy pair of lace undies. "Is it appropriate to meet your mother?"

"Definitely not. We'll spend the night at my house in Crete. I need to have the boat checked after its maiden voyage." In other words, searched for bugs and cameras. "We can pick up a few things for you before we head to Gavdos tomorrow."

"So soon? Couldn't we stay in Crete for a week or so?" Give her time to escape.

"No. You can't put off meeting your new mother-in-law forever, *glykia mou*. And don't worry, she'll love you as much as I do." His words were not reassuring, considering he didn't love her at all.

She shrugged, trying not to think about meeting Demetri's family. Would they consider her a scheming bitch who'd snared their only son? Or welcome her with open arms as a woman to make him happy? There was nothing she could do but be herself, so no point worrying. Pulling on a pair of shorts and a loose top, she forced her eyes not to linger on Demetri who looked sexier than ever with his tousled hair, morning stubble, and sleepy eyes.

"I'm going to exercise. I'll see you at breakfast." She left before she could change her mind and climb back into bed.

Forty minutes later, Demetri sauntered onto the deck where she was stretching after her workout. The cool breeze off the sea as the boat plowed toward Crete felt wonderful on her skin. Unfortunately, it wasn't enough to prevent the heat that engulfed her as Demetri's gaze swept over her contorted body. Drenched in sweat, her hair plastered to her head, she could imagine the sight she presented, whereas he was ultra-sexy with his still damp hair, navy shorts, and white shirt with the top two buttons undone.

"I'm off to take a shower," she mumbled before fleeing his presence once again.

Who the hell am I? Rania Ghalli didn't run from men. She also didn't run from desire. She was discrete, but took her pleasure when she wanted, which hadn't been too often lately, with the worry over her uncle. So why was she hesitating with Demetri? Was it more than lust? Couldn't be. Because as grateful as she was for how he'd bailed her out with the Egyptian agents, she was still annoyed about the way he'd coerced her into a very real marriage.

If she had to marry him, she was going to do it in style. Rania style.

• • •

Demetri lounged on the sofa, sipped champagne, and waited for Rania to parade before him in the next evening gown. He hadn't shopped with many women, preferring to hand over a wad of cash and wait for them to appear later with a selection of bags and put on a private show for him. With Rania he couldn't guarantee she wouldn't bolt as soon as she was out of his sight. So he'd been forced to come with her. However it was proving to be more enjoyable than he'd expected, especially once he'd instructed the shop assistants to select more provocative attire.

"I'm not coming out wearing this," Rania said from inside the change room.

"Shall I come in?" he replied.

"Damn you to hell, Demetri Christodoulou," she said through obviously clenched teeth. "This is the very last one I'm trying on. You know perfectly well I'll never wear any of these dresses. I've looked up Gavdos on your computer. There's nothing there except a small café. And don't tell me your family dresses this way for dinner because I won't believe you."

"Show me the dress, Rania. I'll decide if it's appropriate. And we won't spend all our time on Gavdos. I have business on the other islands and dinners to attend with investors. As my wife…"

Rania emerged from the room, and Demetri swallowed. He'd thought her bikini provocative. Just because there was more fabric didn't mean the dress was less enticing. It had seemed nice on the hanger. Rania made it gorgeous. A deep green color, it brought out the copper tones in her hair and the gold flecks in her eyes. It also hugged her curves and the see-through panels assured the viewer that the wearer wasn't enhanced by artificial support. Rania slowly turned. Her back was entirely bare, the dress dipping to the base of her spine in soft folds. It was perfect. She was perfect.

"We'll take it," he managed to say. However he'd reached his limit on public displays of Rania's body, at least until he'd had his fill of private exhibitions. He called an end to the fashion show.

"I can pay for my own clothes," Rania argued when they sat in the limo twenty minutes later. "All I wanted was a few more T-shirts and shorts and maybe a pair of jeans for when it gets colder. This fancy dress thing was all your fault."

He glanced over and couldn't stop his smile when he saw her pout. "You are the first woman I've met who gets upset when a man buys her clothes. Every other woman I've known couldn't wait for me to get my wallet out."

"Let's get one thing clear between us, Demetri. I am not like any other woman you have met, dated, or slept with. The sooner you understand that I can't be bought, intimidated, or wowed with money, the easier this relationship will be. I will pay you back for all the clothes. Except the last dress. You can keep that one and pass it on to the next Mrs. Christodoulou."

She had a point. She wasn't like any other woman. So he'd have to come up with new ways of dealing with her. Until he'd secured the property and had his fill, that was.

"What do you want to eat? If you're tired of Greek food, there's a good French restaurant I know." He'd enjoy walking into Calypso with Rania on his arm.

"If we can stop for a few groceries, I'm sure I can make something edible. I've eaten out for the past month. I wouldn't mind something home cooked."

She cooked? Would a year be enough to get to know this woman? He instructed the driver to stop at the nearest market and half an hour later he was in awe. The excitement he'd expected to see as she'd entered the exclusive boutiques he'd taken her to was now on her face as she chatted with a stall owner about the freshness of her produce. After an animated discussion in combined English and some other language he didn't know, she handed him another bag.

"All we need now is a loaf of fresh bread. I assume you have wine at home?"

"I have wine." He had a cellar full of some of the world's

best wines. He didn't think she'd be impressed by that.

She wasn't impressed by his house either. It had six bedrooms and sat on the cliff face with an amazing view of the bay, especially from the infinity pool. The two other women he'd brought here had almost salivated at the thought of living in the prestigious property. Rania had only asked for the location of the kitchen leaving him to bring in her bags of clothes and shoes. It took three trips.

The clatter of pans and cupboard doors being opened and closed led him to her. Rania had pulled her hair up and secured it with two chopsticks. Every burner on the stove had a pot on it and already an enticing aroma permeated the air.

"What can I do?" He resisted the urge to take her in his arms. He was hungry, but other appetites had awakened seeing her bustling about the kitchen. Her hips circled in concert with the whisk in the bowl she was stirring.

"Are you any good?"

He raised an eyebrow at her question and she laughed. "In the kitchen. Are you any good in the kitchen?" she clarified quickly.

"While I admit it's not my best room, performance wise, I've been known to prepare an edible meal." It was beans on toast, but he was alive. That had to count.

"I don't think your boardroom prowess will help us here."

He smirked at her comment and undid a button on his shirt. "That's not my best room either."

She stuck her tongue out at him and he sucked in a deep breath. Playful banter was new to him. Most of his previous women had been refined to the point of stuck-up. Rania was a breath of fresh air—intoxicating, addictive air.

"You can be sous-chef, then," she said. "First, I need two bottles of wine, white for cooking, whatever you prefer for drinking."

He went to select a couple bottles from his cellar,

returning a few minutes later. "Do you like to cook to music?" He poured two glasses of merlot and uncorked the white for her to use in the cooking. Rania moved around the kitchen as though she'd cooked there for years. She splashed a generous amount of wine into a sizzling pan with a mixture of mushrooms. His mouth watered.

"Sure. Anything but rap. It makes me dizzy trying to figure out what they're saying."

"No rap. Sade okay?"

"You really are old school in your music taste."

"I prefer the term classic. The relatives I lived with in England were both jazz musicians. I guess their musical preference rubbed off on me. But I can download something else if you'd rather."

"No jazz is cool. My dad likes it as well."

"Not sure I want to be categorized with your father," he said. "I'll update my playlist tomorrow with Ed Sheeran and Taylor Swift."

"Ha, I knew you were a secret Swiftie."

He laughed and put the music on, then spent a few minutes admiring the symphony of Rania's movements as she chopped, stirred, and tasted. Her body moved to the music in an unconscious seduction and again he resisted the urge to touch her. He had to clear his throat before he could speak. "What else can I do?"

"Slice the bread, spread this on it, and then toast it lightly under the grill." He did as she asked, and ten minutes later they sat on the deck, enjoying a mushroom medley on herb buttered toast. It was one of the best things he'd eaten in months.

The rest of the delicious meal followed as Rania prepared it. The main course was grilled lamb on skewers, with a yogurt dip different enough from tzatziki to tantalize his jaded taste buds. When she produced a molten lava cake for dessert, he called her out.

"Are you trying to prove some sort of super wife credentials?"

"No way. You force me to marry you, you get what you get. I enjoy cooking and haven't done much lately with my travels. I would make this meal for any of my sisters and their husbands or my parents. It's one of my favorites."

"You have a large family?" If there were so many of them, why was she was the one trying to rescue her uncle?

"I'm the youngest of four girls. My sisters are married, and they all live in Canada now. My parents are in London at the moment. Dad is an antiquities expert and is accompanying the touring pharaohs museum exhibition. Uncle Fouad sensed the winds of change years ago and urged us to relocate out of the country. He stayed behind to run his business."

"Why isn't your father the one trying to free your uncle?"

"Have you seen any of the Indiana Jones films?"

Non sequitur question, but he'd play along. "Of course."

"You know the character Marcus Brody, the scatter-brained archaeologist who once got lost in his own museum?"

He nodded.

"That's my father. He's a brilliant man. He can name every pharaoh and give the dates of their reign and minute details about their lives. Yet he can't remember my birthday or my middle name."

"What is your middle name?"

"Safiya. Rania Safiya Ghalli."

"Christodoulou, as of next week."

A shadow crossed her face and a stab of guilt pricked his conscience. Before it could overpower his desire for Rania he returned to the subject of her family. "What about your brothers-in-law? Have they tried to get your uncle out of prison? Surely your sisters must be worried as well?"

"They've made a token effort, but my uncle and I have

a special bond. He was married to my mother's sister so he's an uncle by marriage not blood. My aunt died in childbirth, along with the baby. I was born a week later, and my uncle has always considered me as the child he should have had. I was supposed to work for him and eventually take over his construction company. I guess none of that will happen now." She worried her bottom lip with her teeth.

Tears glistened in her eyes and his chest tightened. He reached out a hand to touch her. "Rania—"

Instead of accepting his comfort, she stood. "I'll clean up. What time do you want to set off in the morning?"

"Leave the dishes. I have a cleaning service. They'll come tomorrow and sort everything out. And we'll depart when we're ready. That's why I bought the boat, so I could leave when it suited me. Sail time to Gavdos is about five hours. As long as we get there before dark, we're fine."

"Okay then. Which bedroom should I use?"

"Mine?" She raised both eyebrows and waited for him to stand. He took her hand and led her back into the house, up the stairs then down the hall. "You can have the room next to mine. I have an alarm system, so if you try to escape, it will alert the whole neighborhood." Although the nearest neighbor was half a kilometer away and he didn't fancy explaining to the police why his alleged new wife had run away in the middle of the night.

"I won't leave."

He opened a door to one of the guest rooms and waited for her to enter. Her shopping bags were piled at the end of the bed. "There's a bathroom through that door. It should be stocked with towels and necessities. If you need anything, or want to sleep on top of someone, I'm next door."

"I'll be fine here. Thank you."

"Rania."

"Yes?"

"We're going to have a good marriage, for as long as it lasts. We seem to get along well, and I'll do my best to make you happy."

"How can I be happy knowing my marriage has an expiration date?" Before he could respond, she drew in a deep breath. "I'll see you in the morning, Demetri. Good night."

He closed the door behind him and returned to the patio, too restless to sleep yet. Was he doing the right thing, forcing Rania into marriage? It benefited them both, so it made business sense. When he looked in her eyes, it wasn't business he was thinking about.

A warm breeze brought the scent of the sea with it. Born and raised until the age of twelve on a small island, he had as much salt as blood in his veins. Then his grandfather had exiled him to London, hoping his relocation would erase the stain Demetri's birth had brought on the family name.

His cousins in London had provided him with a loving home, and he couldn't complain about his treatment or his life in the UK. But he'd gone to bed every night longing for the smell of the sea and his mother's smile. He'd promised himself that one day he would return to Gavdos triumphant, and make sure his grandfather knew that his embarrassment of a bastard grandson had made more of the family name than the old man ever had.

The woman sleeping in the room next to his was the key to accomplishing that. It was the other things her key might inadvertently open up that worried him.

• • •

Demetri glanced into the shoebox the security expert showed him. There were at least twenty listening devices and seven miniature cameras in it.

"We've done a triple check. The boat is clean now of

surveillance devices. The only way to ensure there isn't a GPS tracker somewhere is to have the boat pulled out of the water entirely. Some of the stuff we found is high quality, more than what you'd find commercially available. The cheap, dummy ones we found easily. They're what we call decoys and are meant to be found so the person thinks they're safe. It took six hours to locate all the others. The person who planted this equipment really wants to know what you're up to. I suggest you allow me to check your phone and your wife's, too."

It no longer surprised him to hear Rania referred to as his wife, perhaps because he'd begun to think of her as that as well. Eight more days and she would be.

Demetri handed over his phone and called to Rania. It was noon, and they were due to depart in less than an hour. She'd been quiet all morning, not saying anything as they filed the papers for their marriage license. Now all they had to do was post a notice of their intent to marry once they reached Gavdos and over a week later they could be wed. As Rania had been baptized as a Coptic Christian, they could even be married in the church. His mother and grandmother would be ecstatic.

His fingertips tingled but he wasn't sure if it was the thought of finally getting his hands on the land, or on Rania. He'd decided last night, as he'd tossed and turned in frustrated desire, that he'd wait until their wedding night to make love to her. Then, in the event of an accidental pregnancy, there would be no question of him producing a bastard. One in the family was enough.

Still, as she approached him, he sucked in a breath. Even dressed in a T-shirt and shorts, she exuded a sexuality that made his blood flow south, and not for the first time that day he wondered whether he'd be able to wait eight more days.

He had to clear his throat before he could speak. "Rania, Terry wants to check your phone for spyware."

She passed her phone to him, careful to make sure their hands didn't touch. "I have a bit of a headache. I'm going to lie down for a while."

He searched her features. She did look a bit pale. "All right, *glykia mou*. If you need anything, use the phone in the room to call the captain, and he'll send someone to find me."

She nodded then disappeared. Terry rattled the box with the disabled spy equipment, and Demetri pulled himself out of his latest Rania-filled fantasy.

"I know it's none of my business, Mr. Christodoulou, but this was a professional job done on your boat...and your wife's phone is compromised. You may want to consider hiring additional security. It may be more than information they're after."

"Thank you. I'll take your suggestion under advisement." They'd be safe enough on Gavdos. He knew all the residents there and the handful of tourists who were still on the island this late in the season would be easy enough to keep track of. Few of them ventured to where his family lived anyway, preferring the sandy beaches and close access to facilities on the other side of the island.

"If you need any recommendations, don't hesitate to call me. Just don't use this phone." Terry handed Rania's mobile back. "It would be better to get a brand new phone for your wife. I can't guarantee they won't be able to reactivate the spyware on this one. If you know what this is all about, you could use this phone to spread false information."

Terry's words solidified the suspicions in Demetri's mind. Whoever Rania's uncle was, he was more than a lowly political prisoner. He wanted to make sure his *wife* was who she said she was as well, so he'd asked his lawyer to hire someone to investigate both of them. The report was due the day before the wedding. He sure as hell hoped it had good news.

In the meantime, Demetri had his hands full of women.

Despite his reassurances to Rania, he wasn't completely sure how his mother and grandmother were going to take to her. He also had to break the news to Christina that he was marrying someone else and manage her disappointment without ruining the friendship between their families. It was her uncle who was selling the land, and he needed her to understand that she was better off without him. And then there was Rania, a woman he desperately wanted, liked more than he'd expected, and wasn't sure he could trust.

The next week would be the most crucial of his life.

Chapter Five

Rania held on to the railing as the boat docked in the tiny harbor on Gavdos. Demetri came up behind her and put his arms around her waist. She leaned her head back on his chest as he kissed her temple. This relationship may have an expiration date, but it didn't mean she couldn't eek out every last minute of pleasure until it hit the "best before" deadline.

"How's your headache?"

"Better, thanks. Is your family expecting us?"

"Yes, my mother has already called and reamed me out for not telling her first about our *marriage*. I appeased her by telling her we would have another ceremony here next week. So she shouldn't be too upset when you meet her."

Rania tried to picture Demetri's mother. Was she a widow who wore black year in year out, mourning the death of her one true love? Or was she a bitter divorcée who would think no woman good enough for her son?

"You never speak of your father." And there had been nothing on the Internet about him either.

Demetri stiffened behind her and for a moment she didn't

think he would answer. "My father was a Turkish fisherman who got stranded on the island for two weeks during a series of severe storms. He and my mother had a brief affair. By the time she realized she was pregnant, dear dad was long gone. She was only seventeen." His voice was tight with barely restrained emotion.

She turned in his arms and put a hand on his cheek, caressing the throbbing muscle in his jaw with her thumb. "Your poor mom. Did she never get in touch with him? Let him know he had a son?"

"My grandfather forbade it. Said I was enough of a dishonor on the family name. He didn't want a deadbeat Turkish son-in-law as well."

She kissed Demetri lightly on the lips, tasting his disdain. "Is your grandfather still alive?"

"Yes."

"Then he's in for a shock when he meets me, because I think you're the making of the Christodoulou name. Not many men would have answered the plea of a stranger rather than surrendering her to armed gunmen."

"A naked stranger," he said.

"I figured that might persuade you. I was just going to crawl into the bed, then I figured the shower was a nicer touch."

"Definitely a nicer touch." His hands ran up her back and into her hair, which she'd left loose for a change. He angled her head and then his lips descended. The kiss was gentle, persuasive, but as she kissed him back it soon turned passionate. Her hand found its way to his hair, the other toyed with the buttons on his shirt, undoing one before moving on to the next.

An angry male voice speaking Greek interrupted her exploration of Demetri's chest. She buried her face against his shirt for a moment, trying to catch her breath.

"Good evening, *Pappous*. Where are Ma and *Yiayia*?" Demetri said in English.

"At home creating a meal to welcome your bride. I am glad they were not here to see you make such a spectacle." Demetri's grandfather's English was heavily accented but clear, his tone gruff and unbending.

Every muscle in Demetri's body clenched. Rania turned and took a step away. A gnarled old man stood with his arms across his chest, his feet planted apart. From the corner of her eye, she noticed Demetri had the same stance.

The crew had tied the boat up while she and Demetri had been engaged in their kiss and placed a small gangplank to bridge the distance between boat and dock. Rania descended and approached the older man.

"Hi, I'm Rania. I'm pleased to meet you, Mr. Christodoulou. Demetri has told me nothing about you so I must learn it all for myself." She linked her arm with his and started walking toward the end of the pier, leaving Demetri to follow after. Or not. "For example," she continued, "do you object to all public displays of affection, or only those involving your grandson?"

Pappous grunted a non-committal reply.

"Well, we'll try to keep our hands, and lips, to ourselves when you're around. You must remember what it's like with newlyweds. Demetri has a photo of his *yiayia* at the house in Crete. She's a beautiful woman. I'm sure you had a difficult time controlling your affections, probably even now. I've been told that in a good marriage passion doesn't die, it gets stronger. Would you agree, *Pappous*?"

"My marriage is very good," he said almost reluctantly.

Rania glanced back at the boat. Demetri still stood on deck, arms crossed. "Are you coming, *habibi*? We don't want to keep your mother and grandmother waiting." His heavy steps on the dock behind them sounded like thunder.

His grandfather led her over to an old Jeep and opened the door for her. Demetri jumped in the back and they sped off in a spurt of gravel. She held on for dear life. The tension in the vehicle was palpable as not a word was exchanged between grandfather and grandson. Not exactly the warm welcome she'd been hoping for. Maybe the reception from Demetri's mother and grandmother would be friendlier.

Pappous pulled up in front of a respectable, one-story house set halfway up a hill. In the fading light, Rania could see a beautiful bay with a crescent-shaped beach below. The lowering sun gave the sand a golden glow. As she stared, amazed at the view, Demetri came up to her and slid his hand into hers.

"Ready?"

She smiled up at him. He squeezed her hand but didn't lean down to kiss her. Their gazes locked until the front door of the house flung open. Demetri glanced toward the residence, and his face creased into a smile of love. Rania caught her breath at the transformation; a fluttery feeling invaded her chest. A woman in her late forties raced over and wrapped her arms around him. He released Rania's hand and returned his mother's hug.

"Ma, let me introduce you to Rania."

A flurry of Greek followed from the woman, interspersed with tears. Rania found it difficult to follow the emotional outburst. Eventually, the woman released Demetri and appraised her.

Rania swallowed. This marriage may be pretend, but it suddenly felt very real.

• • •

Demetri saw his mother eye-up Rania. He hadn't introduced his family to many of his previous girlfriends, preferring to keep his romantic relationships separate from his familial ones. He reached out and encouraged Rania to come closer.

"Rania, this is my mother, Maria. Ma, this is my wife, Rania."

He'd been impressed with the way Rania had dealt with his grandfather, not letting his criticism get to her. In fact, she'd turned the tables on the old man, shown him she wouldn't be bullied. His mother, however, would require a different touch. He should have told Rania more about his one parent, but he was curious as to how she would handle the situation.

The two women embraced before Rania returned almost naturally to his side. "May I call you Ma?" she asked. "My mom is traveling with my father and hasn't been living near me for the past two years. I miss having someone to give me motherly advice."

Clever play. His mother nodded.

"And I have to apologize to you," Rania added. "I was so excited to marry Demetri I didn't stop to think about how you would feel, not being present at your son's wedding. I'm not a mother—yet," she paused for dramatic effect, "but I know I wouldn't be happy if my son showed up with a ready-made bride. I hope you can forgive me and allow the wedding here to make up for my hasty actions earlier this week."

"Well, I'm sure you weren't the only one to blame," his mother said.

Rania laughed. "No, Demetri didn't put up much of a fight when I suggested we marry immediately. As a woman, I should have thought about the consequences of our actions on others," Rania replied.

He didn't know whether to be impressed or insulted. However, at the smile that creased his mother's face he figured Rania knew exactly what she was doing. "Yes, men only think about the wedding night."

Rania actually blushed. She was one amazing actress.

He'd have to remember that. In truth, he didn't know how much he should trust her. And while he was willing to share his life, and especially his bed with her, he'd keep his heart under close guard.

"You must be hungry," his mother said. "Come inside."

He let go of Rania, and she followed his mother into the tiny house. His grandfather sat on his usual chair on the porch, waiting for the call that dinner was ready. From where he sat, he'd have a prime view of the resort Demetri planned to build. It couldn't come soon enough.

"Interesting woman you have married." His grandfather's gruff voice broke through Demetri's daydream. "At least you did it the right way around, got married first. Unless she is already with child and that is why you did not wait. Your ma and *yiayia* were very upset when you called."

"Rania is not pregnant. And I'll make it up to Ma and *Yiayia*."

His grandfather grunted again, and Demetri's hands clenched into fists.

"You can have the house I bought for when your mother married, although I doubt you will stay on Gavdos. Young people these days are more interested in clubs and fancy restaurants than preserving the heritage of their family."

"We'll live mostly in Crete or Athens. It has nothing to do with clubs and fancy restaurants though. I run a multinational business with a turnover of 160 million euros, *Pappous*. I can't do that from this tiny island."

If he hoped his grandfather would be impressed, he was again disappointed. It'd be better to spend his time with people who actually loved him. He wandered into the house and could hear Rania in the kitchen with his mother and grandmother. She laughed at something his *yiayia* said and the other two women chuckled with her. In less than three minutes she'd integrated herself into his family.

Rania asked for further instructions on whatever they were making, her Greek a little mispronounced but perfectly understandable. It halted him on his way to the kitchen. Rania understood Greek? What else was she hiding? Was this all a setup? His scam-o-meter kicked up another notch.

The real marriage had been his idea, hadn't it? From the doorway, he admired Rania's nimble fingers as she followed his grandmother's directions in folding the spanakopita pastry. Soon those fingers would be roving over his body. Heat engulfed him. Forget waiting eight days; they'd start their honeymoon tonight.

"Oh, Demetri, I didn't see you there," his mother said. Rania shot him a subtle smile as if to say she'd noticed him watching her and had a pretty good idea what he'd been thinking. His mother continued. "I was just suggesting that Rania stay here with us. We have so much to do to organize a wedding in eight days."

"I…" He'd vowed years ago he wouldn't sleep another night under his grandfather's roof. And even if he did, the walls were so thin there was no way he'd be able to do all the things he wanted to Rania. "We'll stay on my yacht. We can moor it in the bay—"

"Demetri, don't be ridiculous," Rania said. "We should stay with your family."

He narrowed his eyes. What game was she playing now?

"You stay on your boat. Rania stays with us," *Yiayia* declared.

"I didn't get married to sleep alone." Last night had been hard enough.

Rania opened her mouth but there wasn't a lot she could say. It wasn't as if she could tell his mother and grandmother they weren't actually married. He thought he'd won the argument, then his grandmother put her hands on her hips. "Until the priest blesses your marriage, you are not married in God's eyes. Or mine. Rania will sleep here. You will stay on your boat."

Rania's eyes danced with laughter, and she struggled to keep her face straight in an appropriate penitent expression as she murmured, "Yes, *Yiayia*."

Demetri clenched his teeth so tight his jaw ached.

All through dinner, Rania kept his family entertained. She made up a story of their first meeting, as they both tried to hail the same taxi in Tirana, then of them canceling their respective meetings to have dinner together instead. Culminating in his proposal on a beach, three days later as they were both due to leave Albania, begging her to stay with him forever. Demetri's mother wiped a tear from her eye, his grandmother looked like she might melt, and even his grandfather's face had a trace of a smile, the first Demetri had seen in years. It was a good story, but it had nothing on the reality of her pressing her naked body against his in the shower on his yacht. That made him smile.

"Demetri, don't you think you should go see Christina?" His mother's words wiped the smile off his face.

"Yes, I'd better. I'll say goodnight to Rania first." He walked out on the porch. The sea breeze ruffled his hair and filled his nose with the salty smell of his early childhood, until Rania put her arms around his waist and her intoxicating fragrance filled his senses. She was addictive. If they'd have met as she'd told his family, it was quite possible that he'd have asked her to marry him, eventually.

"Do you want me to come with you?"

Christina. Damn. "No, I'd better see her alone."

"I'm sorry. I didn't mean for anyone to get hurt. If you think she can keep a secret, maybe you can tell her our relationship is only temporary."

He considered it for a second. "No. I think it would be even crueler to keep her waiting another year." Holding

Rania in his arms, her lush curves pressed against him, he couldn't contemplate marriage to Christina any longer.

"Until tomorrow then." She stood on tiptoe and pressed a quick kiss against his cheek.

"No one is watching. We can kiss properly."

"If no one is watching, there's no need."

"There's always a need." To emphasize his point he pressed her even closer to his growing erection. Eight days couldn't come soon enough.

Her laugh echoed through the darkness. Before she could come up with another excuse he caught her lips with his own. She tasted faintly of the ouzo she'd sipped after dinner. As their tongues dueled, he slid a hand up her back, tangling in her long hair. The other was making its way around to cup her breast. The porch light flickered on and off, then on and off again.

For God's sake, I'm a grown man kissing my alleged wife. Not a horny teenager making out with the neighbor's daughter.

"Seems someone was watching after all. I guess that's our cue to wrap things up," Rania murmured against his chest. She was breathing rapidly, her breasts rubbing tantalizingly against his chest. He wasn't anywhere close to wrapping this up.

"You could come stay with me on the yacht…"

"Patience, *habibi*. Good things come to those who wait."

Much more waiting and I'll come all too soon.

"Good night, *glykia mou*." He released her while he still had some control over his body.

She slipped inside the house and he trudged over to the Jeep. He wasn't looking forward to breaking Christina's heart.

Ten minutes later he knocked gently on her parents' door. When she answered, her face was blotchy and her lashes still damp. It didn't surprise him that word of his arrival with another woman had reached her already. He should have come straight here.

"I'm sorry, Christina," he said.

"You never promised me anything. I just assumed…" Her voice broke and she buried her face again in a tissue. If this were Rania he'd disappointed, he would probably be facing a fierce verbal and physical assault. Tears were harder to deal with.

"No, it's all my fault. You are a sweet, beautiful woman. I never meant to lead you on. I did think we would get together. Then I met Rania and my whole world was turned upside down." He didn't lie.

"I understand."

"I hope you'll find happiness with a man worthy of you, Christina."

"Thank you." She closed the door, and he heard a fresh bout of weeping.

His stomach clenched. He wasn't really surprised by her reaction. If it were Rania he'd broken up with, the encounter would have been much more passionate. A year from now when their marriage ended, would he be sporting a black eye? Or would they part with a handshake and a promise to remain friends?

A chill swept through his body at the idea of leaving Rania, even a year from now. His phone pinged with an incoming text, and he glanced at it before starting the Jeep for the short drive back to the harbor.

Thought you might want to know, I'm completely naked in YOUR old bed. Good night. The Wife.

It was going to be an interesting year.

• • •

Rania stared at the shack in front of her. The roof had massive holes. There was no front door and she was pretty sure a couple of goats had already set up home in it. "You have got to be kidding me."

Rather than look at the ruin, Demetri watched her. "Did you assume that marrying a wealthy man meant you were going to live in luxury?"

"I assumed that any house I'd live in, no matter who I married, would have a roof…and a door."

"We'll fix it up before we move in, and we won't spend all our time here." He shrugged as though living in a goat shed was perfectly normal. "I'm not living with my grandparents and mother. And the boat has to go in for a service after its maiden voyage."

There was something he wasn't telling her. "And there's nothing else on the island to buy or rent?"

"This is it. My grandfather bought it when my mother was a child for when she got married."

"Your grandfather didn't like your mother either?"

Demetri laughed but there wasn't a lot of humor in it. She noticed he tensed every time his grandfather was near or even mentioned. "I assume it was in a lot better shape when he bought it. And I guess he gave up caring for it years ago when it became evident she wasn't getting married."

"Why didn't she ever marry? Surely some people are open minded enough to accept her with a child."

"I never really asked. I have a feeling she still holds the dream that one day my father will come back. I heard her crying once when I was young, saying she'll never love another man the way she loved him."

Rania turned back to stare at the shack. She had to remember that her marriage to Demetri was temporary. The last thing she wanted was to end up like his mother, loving a man who left and never came back. It was all right to have fun and enjoy her time with the gorgeous man next to her. It wasn't all right to fall in love with him.

"How are your goat-wrangling skills?" she asked as a shaggy animal with long horns stood in the doorway, barring them from entering.

"About as good as my cooking."

"Heaven help us, then."

Demetri took off his shirt and started waving it at the goat. It looked at him with disdain. Heaving a huge sigh, Rania rolled up her sleeves and prepared to get her new home habitable.

Hours later, the goats had been evicted and the rooms swept out. It was going to take some pretty powerful disinfectant to get rid of the smell. Demetri's mother had arrived ten minutes ago and brought them a picnic lunch, so they sat at the top of the hill, eating last night's lamb roast in a pita pocket. Demetri's body glistened with sweat, highlighting his muscled torso. Too bad his mother was around.

"At least the view is fabulous," Rania said, looking for the positive in the realization that this was her new home. The Mediterranean was deep blue in the distance, changing through a myriad of shades as it approached the sandy beaches. A little further down the hill, she spied Demetri's grandmother working in her vegetable patch at the back of the house. His yacht was moored in the bay below, the sun gleaming off the white hull, almost blinding her.

"I agree." Rather than checking out the view, he was staring at her.

His mother started to pack up her lunch. "You don't need to go, Ma," Rania quickly said.

Maria stood and brushed a few crumbs off her jeans. "I think you two want to be alone, without an old woman for company. I remember…" There was an odd hitch in her voice before her words drifted off.

"You're not old," Demetri said. Before he could add

more, his cell phone rang.

"Ma, I'd love your opinion on what we could do to make the house livable." Rania stood and the two women made their way back down to the shack, leaving Demetri to his phone call, which didn't sound like good news judging from the few expletives he'd muttered as the caller spoke.

"This is where Burak and I came to be together. Demetri was conceived on a small bed that used to be over in the corner," Maria said, her voice distant.

"I'm sorry. I didn't realize…"

Great, Rania, rub the woman's unhappiness in her face.

"No, I'm happy you and Demetri will be here, at least for a little while. I have only good memories of this place. I'm sure, once we clean it up, get a new roof, and a door, this will be a good place for you, too. Maybe even my grandchild will be conceived here."

A baby was definitely not part of the plan. "Maybe." Before she could say more, Demetri strode through the door. The tiny house suddenly seemed made for intimacy. With no neighbors within earshot, except a few goats, they could make all the noise they wanted.

"I have to leave." Demetri's statement and the finality of his tone sent a cold chill through her.

Chapter Six

Demetri stood at the front of his yacht and stared at the tiny dot on the horizon that was the island of Gavdos. Even though the captain had the engines on maximum speed, it still was taking ages. For the first time in years, Demetri was excited to be going home. And with Rania on the island it seemed like home.

He should have taken her with him when he left, but he knew he'd be distracted by the crisis he'd had to deal with. He'd worried Rania would take advantage and run away to try and get her uncle free. At least on Gavdos, with half the island watching her, she'd be safe. Still, it would have been nice to hold her and listen to her stories at the end of each of the past seven hellish days.

A couple who had been vacationing at one of his resorts had had a violent dispute and the husband had killed the wife before taking his own life. It had been a media nightmare, not to mention the various law enforcement agencies he'd had to deal with. Thankfully, as it was shoulder season, the resort hadn't been at full capacity and he'd been able to move all the other guests to alternative resorts. With the transfer costs and upgrades it hadn't been cheap but he considered it money well spent to keep customer goodwill and his company's reputation high. The emotional toll on his staff would be the next thing to address. He'd already given the cleaning woman who had found the bodies a month's paid leave and provided unlimited counseling sessions.

At the moment, he had the emotions of someone closer to home to worry about. Although he'd called or texted her each day, he was pretty sure Rania was pissed at having been abandoned with a derelict house to fix up. Not to mention being left to deal with his mother and grandmother, crazed with wanting to put on the best wedding the island had ever seen. He'd had ten emails and four voicemails from his mother alone reminding him to bring his best suit when he returned. Rania, on the other hand, had only asked if he had any objection to the color fuchsia. Another surprise. He hadn't pegged her for a girly-girl who liked pink, but if it made her happy, he didn't care what color the decorations were.

Tomorrow they would be married, and he'd start on convincing her that his way to free her uncle was best. For God's sake, her uncle was Fouad Boutros. He owned one of the largest construction companies in the Southern Mediterranean, although he had scaled back his contracts in the past five years. No wonder the Egyptian government was keen to keep him behind bars. His wealth made him a prime political mover, and Rania was widely held to be his next of kin, the main heiress to his fortune, provided the government didn't seize all his assets first.

Demetri's lawyer had made contact with the prison where Fouad Boutros was being held. Negotiations would be tricky, and as Rania had predicted, probably cost a shit-load of money. Demetri hoped he could get her uncle free before she came up with another half-assed plan.

The background report on Rania herself had raised more questions than it had answered. She held a degree in environmental engineering, a handy subject given the expectation that she would eventually take over her uncle's company, although such a detail-oriented occupation seemed at odds with her spontaneous personality. There was much more depth to the woman than he'd first assumed. He couldn't wait to unravel her layers.

According to the report, her employers had all said she was very skilled and creative in finding solutions to issues. The only problem was she never stayed longer than two years. In fact, for the past six months, she hadn't worked at all but rather traveled around Europe and the Black Sea. Her personal life was a complete mystery with no mention of past boyfriends or lovers. He'd have to discover her secrets himself. At least she didn't have a criminal record, not one they'd been able to uncover anyway.

The island finally loomed larger on the horizon and Demetri went below deck to get ready to meet his bride-to-be. The thrill that raced through him must be due to the proximity of their wedding night. It was definitely something to look forward to.

When he reemerged onto the deck, they were pulling into the harbor. Demetri scanned the dock hoping to see Rania waiting for him; he'd called ahead and given her an estimated time of arrival. He shoved down the disappointment when he couldn't spot her. As his crew tied the boat to the wharf, a large contingency of the island's male population abandoned their lively backgammon games at the café next to the harbor. They formed an odd welcoming party at the end of the pier. Were they going to throw him a stag party? Demetri released a loud groan. He'd rather spend the evening with Rania, finding out how her week had been, holding her, imagining all the things he'd do to her in twenty-four hours.

Demetri waited for the crew to secure the gangplank before making his way toward the assembled crowd. His grandfather's closest friend Kosta stood at the end of the dock. "Demetri, we need a word with you." Behind him were Christina's father, the owner of the café where his mother worked part-time, and half a dozen other men who were long-time inhabitants of the island.

"If it's about the wedding, I have no idea what my mother and grandmother have arranged," Demetri said.

"It's about your woman. You need to get her in line," Christina's father replied.

"My woman?" If they knew Rania at all, they wouldn't dare call her that in her presence.

"Your wife," Kosta clarified, as if there were so many women in Demetri's life he'd lost track. "She's been disrupting the whole island while you've been gone. You need to get her in line. And next time you leave, take her with you."

He'd been gone seven days. What could Rania have done in that time to necessitate a mob of angry men descending on him as soon as his feet touched Gavdos soil?

"What's she done?" Because if she'd climbed into any other man's shower…

"She told my daughter she should go to Athens and get an education," Christina's father said.

"She interfered with the way we do things," Kosta said.

"She told my wife she deserves a new washing machine before I get a new TV."

"She told my daughter that women should have their own life before they get married."

"She convinced your mother to quit her job."

Demetri had been telling his mother for years that she didn't need to work. He was surprised Rania had managed to get the point home so soon.

The litany of complaints continued, and Demetri had

to hide a smile. If they knew how Rania had turned his life upside down in the week and a half he'd known her, they wouldn't ask him to fix their problems.

"Seems to me your issues are with your own women, not mine. Maybe if you listened to them and took their feelings and needs into consideration, they wouldn't need to seek reassurance from Rania."

Demetri pushed his way through the crowd until his grandfather's friend put a bandaged hand on his arm. "You'll be eating your words once you see your house."

He narrowed his eyes but didn't take the bait. "If you're all so upset with my wife, I'll understand if you're not at the wedding tomorrow." Missing an island social event was akin to excommunication.

"Don't worry, son, we'll all be there to see you wed that vortex. My bet is she has you whipped into her dog-boy before the month is out. And then you'll be coming to us for advice." A chorus of laughter greeted that prediction from someone at the back of the crowd.

Demetri swallowed a quick retort. They just didn't know how to handle Rania. No way was he going to give them advice. He took the keys to the family Jeep that Kosta handed him and jogged up to the parked vehicle. He was now very anxious to hear about Rania's week from the woman herself.

Fifteen minutes later, he stopped the truck at the end of the track leading up to the house his grandfather had given them. Even in the fading light he could see it had been painted a shocking shade of pink.

• • •

Rania glanced at the clock as she heard a vehicle on the gravel road below the house. Where had the time gone? It was four o'clock last time she'd checked. She'd planned to meet

Demetri at the dock, surprised at how much she'd missed him in the week he'd been away. Not that she'd had much time to mope. She'd managed to galvanize the islanders and a few of the handy tourists and turned their goat shack into a home fit for newlyweds. Having left all the work to her, Demetri would have to wait until tomorrow night to see it though.

She climbed down from the ladder where she'd been hanging a sheet over the rough wall that hadn't been plastered yet. The bedroom was fashioned after a Bedouin tent but since neither of them would be lying there contemplating the decor, she figured it didn't mattered much what it looked like. At least it was clean and smelled a hell of a lot better than when she'd first seen it.

"You go," Demetri's mother said. "I'll finish up here and meet you at my parents' house."

"Thanks, Ma. Christina, do you need a ride?"

"No, I will walk home. My father is still upset with me for wanting to go to university, so I'm in no hurry to get there."

"He'll come around, especially when he sees how happy you are."

Rania surveyed the room once more. Demetri was in for a shock, and not just when he saw the house. Maria had cut her hair short and now appeared ten years younger. And with the excitement of her coming adventure, she'd lost the lonely, haunted look she'd had when Rania first saw her.

The friendship with Christina had been a welcome surprise. Demetri's ex-girlfriend had brought some food to feed the bevy of workers Rania had recruited to fix up the house. Expecting the woman to be furious with her for stealing her man, Rania had been pleased to find that although Christina had been upset at first, upon further reflection she was actually relieved Demetri hadn't asked her to marry him. Evidently, she found him rather intimidating. Her initial desire to marry him had been more about the prospect of leaving the island. She didn't think he'd support her dream to become a kindergarten teacher. When she'd discovered that, Rania had sat down with her and together they'd planned out the next three years so Christina could achieve her goal.

The *creak* of the newly installed front gate brought Rania back to the present. Other people's dreams were one thing; her reality was walking up the path. She pulled her hair out of the bun and opened the front door, closing it quickly behind her so he couldn't see inside.

"Hello, Demetri." God, he looked fantastic. Her heart rate sped up and her hands went a bit clammy. Maybe Christina was right—maybe he was too much man.

"Pink? You expect me to live in a pink house?"

And there went the magic. She could tape over his mouth. It was only his body she really wanted anyway.

"I don't give a damn where you live. Stay on your precious boat for all I care. I'm living here. In my pink goat shed." She crossed her arms over her chest and waited for his next complaint.

"Is it pink on the inside, too?"

"No."

"Then I guess once I get through the door the outside color won't matter."

He smiled and her anger dissipated. "See, I knew you were a smart man."

"More like desperate. I'm not going to force you into marrying me, though. I destroyed those notes we wrote on the first night we met. I would never turn you over to the Egyptian authorities, but I hope you will agree to go ahead with the wedding tomorrow, considering the other mutual objectives we have."

Not a very romantic proposal, but a damn sight better than his last one. A muscle throbbed in his cheek, and he'd gone all British on her. She'd noticed he did that when he was trying to keep his emotions under control. This marriage meant more to him than he wanted to admit.

"I'll still marry you tomorrow."

The huge smile that creased his face made her heartbeat quicken.

"Come here, *agape mou*. I've missed you."

He called her "my love," and for a minute she wished it was true. But calling her "my way to get a piece of land and ass" probably didn't slip off the tongue as easily, or translate as well to Greek. Unable to deny herself, she stepped into his arms.

His firm lips grazed over hers. He nibbled on her lower lip before plundering her mouth, his tongue challenging hers. He pressed her up against the closed door while his hand slowly traced a path from her hip to the swell of her breast.

"Let's go inside," he whispered against her ear.

"Can't. Your mother and Christina are there, finishing up, and you can't see it until tomorrow, after the wedding. I take it your investigator didn't uncover any misdemeanors in my past so bad you've changed your mind?"

His hands dropped to his side and he stepped back.

"How did you know I had you investigated?"

"I've had several calls from friends and family saying someone had been making inquiries about me. I told them I was applying for a job and my prospective employer was doing a thorough background check."

"I knew nothing about you…"

"I understand." She should tell him about her surveillance of him. Before she could say anything, he kissed her again.

When he finally raised his head, passion blazed in his eyes. "So, if we can't go inside, let's go to my yacht. We can have a nice meal, dance under the stars…"

"I'm afraid I can't do that either. I have to help your grandmother with a little problem."

Demetri's face became concerned. "*Yiayia* has a problem?"

"Not for much longer. If you promise to keep your mouth shut and don't interfere, I'll let you tag along."

"You'll let me tag along?" His eyebrows made it to the center of his forehead.

She loved throwing him off balance. Taking his hand, she started walking toward the Jeep. "If you promise to keep quiet and don't try to stop us."

"Rania, what are you up to?"

"Just protecting your grandmother's interests. Come on, we're going to have a family dinner tonight."

"What about my mother?"

"She said she'll walk down later."

Demetri climbed behind the wheel and stared at Rania for a moment before he started the vehicle. "Why do I get the feeling that the file I have on you is only a listing of irrelevant facts and I'm no closer to knowing you than I was a week ago?"

"Maybe because a dry report can't capture the quirkier side of my personality?"

"Am I going to regret this marriage, Rania?"

She wanted to remind him that the real marriage was his idea. He could still marry some other woman and get his land, and she could find another way to get her uncle free. The thought of saying goodbye, never seeing Demetri again, started a slow burn in her chest.

"I promise you this. I will never do anything intentionally to hurt you or your family. Your mother, your *yiayia*, even your *pappous,* have become as important to me as my own relatives. And I won't play you false. I'll be the best wife you've ever had, but I won't stop being me or trying to help people I care about."

"I can't ask for anything more. And speaking of people

you care about, my lawyer has made contact with the prison holding your uncle. I'm working on his release, Rania. So you don't need to jump into any more men's showers. Trust me to do this for you."

She searched his face. Others had offered to help, only to falter when it got tough. Perhaps Demetri's steely determination would see him through, although she still had doubts that doing things legally was going to get her uncle free.

"As long as you keep me informed, I won't do anything rash, at least not without telling you first."

"I guess that's the best I can hope for with you." He leaned over and gave her a long, lingering kiss. "One more thing," he said.

"Hmmm?"

"Tomorrow, after we're legally married, I get you for twenty-four hours. No quests, no interruptions, no interference. Just you, me, and the inside of this god-awful pink house."

She heaved a weary sigh but couldn't keep the smile off her face. "Oh, all right, then. If you insist."

The lustful look he gave set off a tingle in the back of her thighs. Twenty-four hours of Demetri. What more could a girl ask for? *A lifetime*? The unbidden thought made her frown. She had a year, maybe less if they both got what they wanted from this marriage sooner rather than later. She couldn't risk falling in love with him.

Then again, when he saw what she was going to do tonight, the whole wedding might be called off anyway. Was the twenty-four hour thing contingent on the marriage going ahead?

• • •

Demetri parked the Jeep in front of his grandparents' house. So far, everything seemed normal. At least their house wasn't pink. *Pappous* was sitting in his usual spot on the porch. He looked a little different. And when he greeted Demetri warmly, even standing to hug his grandson, little red flags went up in Demetri's brain.

Thirty years and it was the first time he could remember his grandfather hugging him. What had Rania done? Was his grandfather hopped up on drugs? Before he could ask, Rania kissed his grandfather on both cheeks. Not an air kiss, a physical contact kiss, complete with sound effect. "How was your *nap, Pappous*?"

His grandfather actually blushed. Demetri was afraid to ask what had caused the transformation. A second later, *Yiayia* appeared at the door. Her gray hair was no longer pulled back in a severe bun, but left loose with only the front clipped back. She was even wearing lipstick. Demetri pinched himself to make sure he wasn't dreaming. Was this really his family?

While he stared at his grandmother, his grandfather said, "Welcome home, Demetri. We were sorry to hear about what happened at one of your hotels. Is everything back to normal now?" *Pappous* was taking an interest in his business? Demetri had no idea what was normal any more.

"It's settled down for now. The resort is closed for this week, and I've hired a few counselors to help the staff deal with any issues they may be facing. The rest will come with time."

"Well, I'm glad you made it back for the wedding. Rania, your *yiayia,* and mother have put a lot of effort into making the day special."

"I'm sure it will be a day to remember."

"Rania, can you help me put the finishing touches on dinner?"

"Of course, *Yiayia*."

Rania followed his grandmother back into the house

leaving him with his grandfather on the porch. He was about to join the women when *Pappous* stopped him. "We should talk."

"About what?" With an effort he kept his tone light. If his grandfather dared lecture him on how to run his company, or worse, keep his woman in line, then Demetri didn't want to hear it.

"Your marriage."

"*Pappous…*"

"Sit down, Demetri. I can't talk with you looming over me."

Demetri sat on the edge of the chair next to his grandfather's. He swept his gaze over the bay below, reminding himself of the reason he was going through with this folly in the first place. Except a tiny voice in his head said it was becoming less about the land, and more about the woman. He waited for his grandfather to speak.

"As you have no father, I guess it falls to me to talk to you about the wedding night."

Oh, God, no!

"I know what to do, *Pappous*. It won't be my first time." Talking about sex with his grandfather was not going to happen.

"Yes, but with your wife it's different. You have to be more tender. Remember it's a marathon, not a sprint. You can't only think about your own pleasure—"

"I'm sure I can figure it out. Is there anything else?"

"About Rania…"

Here it comes.

"What about Rania? The rest of the men on the island have already given their opinion of my wife when I docked. I was surprised you weren't there as well."

"That's because I don't agree with them. I think she's what you, and this island, need. She's special and exciting and perfect for you, for us. Don't screw this up, son."

"I'll try my best," Demetri said before standing. When this marriage was over, his family would probably prefer to see Rania than him. "If you'll excuse me, I want to see my bride."

Demetri strode into the house before his grandfather could offer any more pearls of wisdom. Rania was alone in the kitchen, peeling potatoes. Warmth spread through his body at the sight of her. He needed to keep his focus before he lost more than he gained from this marriage.

"Where's *Yiayia*?"

Rania jumped at the sound of his voice. Was she feeling guilty about something? Or nervous about tomorrow? After all, he was as much a mystery to her as she was to him. At least he'd had her investigated. She only knew what she'd learned in the past week from a family he wasn't particularly close to.

"She's gone outside to check on a few things," Rania said as she picked up the potato she'd dropped.

"What have you done to my grandfather?" He leaned against the counter, never taking his gaze from her face.

"What makes you think I've done something to him?" A faint blush stained her cheeks. She was definitely guilt ridden.

"He's nice to me. And, well, he looks different." Demetri couldn't put a finger on it, but something about his grandfather had changed in the week he'd been away.

"I may, or may not, have slipped him something to get the old boy upright, if you know what I mean. With your grandmother's permission, of course. A little sex is bound to make any man see the world in a better light, especially when he hasn't had any for a while."

Demetri did not want to think about his grandparents' sex life. "Isn't that dangerous? You can't go around drugging the man."

She swallowed. What else had she been slipping him?

"Your grandmother approved. She said his heart is fine. He's just had a few… mechanical… difficulties. Besides, if you were him, how would you want to go out? Sitting on the front porch feeling a failure? Or riding your woman on a wave of ecstasy?"

"Rania!" This was worse than talking with his grandfather about the wedding night.

"All I'm saying is it's done him, and your grandmother, a world of good. But my supply is running out. You won't believe what I had to trade with the British tourist to get the four pills he had. Any chance you could go to your doctor and get a prescription? Because *Yiayia* says there's no way *Pappous* will admit to having a problem."

"I will not lie to my doctor to get sex pills for my grandfather."

"I figured you'd say that. Guess I'll have to make a deal with the British plumber."

Yiayia returned before he could ask what Rania meant, and there was no way he was going to carry on the conversation with his grandmother present. He'd been gone a week. What the hell would Rania get up to if he left for a month?

"Everything all set for tonight?" Rania asked *Yiayia*.

His grandmother rubbed her hands together in glee. "Yes, I've got twenty years of pent up rage to get rid of, and I've been practicing for days. Piotr almost caught me this morning. Then I put one of those blue pills in his lunch so…"

La la la la la la la.

"Are you going to bother with the sleeping pill tonight?" Rania cut the potatoes, her knife never hesitating while she discussed drugging his grandfather… God, he hoped it was his grandfather they were discussing.

"What do you think? After this afternoon's activities, I'm pretty sure he'll fall asleep quickly."

"Probably, but we don't want him to wake up in the

middle and ruin everything."

"What are you two planning?" Demetri planted his feet apart and crossed his arms over his chest. It was time to put a stop to this nonsense.

"You mean us three," his mother said from the doorway. At least it was his mother's voice. The beautiful woman who stood at the kitchen door looked nothing like the mother he'd left last week.

"What the hell?"

Chapter Seven

"Demetri, is that any way to greet your mother?"

He was used to his mother being happy when he was home, but she positively glowed. She wore makeup, and her hair... She'd cut it short and styled it so she appeared ten years younger. And hot. First his grandparents having sex, now his mother a hottie...

"Sorry, Ma. You look beautiful. Rania, can we talk in private, please?"

She giggled. "I have no secrets from your mother or *Yiayia*."

"I do. Outside. Now."

She dropped the knife and potato and leaned against the counter. Her eyes were full of laughter and he caught his breath. God, she was gorgeous. "Oh, Demetri. You give me goose bumps when you get all manly—"

Enough. He grabbed her by the waist, threw her over his shoulder and strode out the back door. His mother and *yiayia* burst out laughing. He walked up the hill behind the house until he couldn't hear his mother's laughter anymore, not so far that his pink house blinded him.

He set Rania down on her feet. "What have you done to my family, Rania?"

"Aside from helping your granddad get it up?"

"Yes, and I am going to pretend you didn't just say that. Start with my mother." Because he still couldn't think of his grandparents having a sex life without feeling nauseated.

"Well, as you correctly guessed, your mother never got over your father. For thirty years she's been praying every day that he'll return. Evidently, he told her that as soon as he had his own boat and could support her he'd come back. I told her praying wasn't enough; she needed to get active for God to reward her efforts. I suggested she go to Turkey and search for your dad. Then she'd know for sure if he was worth all her prayers."

"You did what?" He yelled so loud a goat that had been grazing nearby leaped away.

"I offered to go with her. I speak some Turkish. My uncle has a place there we can use as a base. We've already done some preliminary research and it seems your father still lives in the town he told her he came from, near Istanbul. If it is him, he's still single, or at least single now. What has she got to lose?"

"What if he breaks her heart? Tells her it meant nothing, that the affair was only two weeks of fun for a lonely and bored fisherman? What if your information is wrong and he has a wife and three children?"

"Then your mother will finally realize he wasn't worthy of her devotion and get on with her life. Do you want her to be sad and lonely forever? She's forty-eight. There's still plenty of time for her to find a man to love and have a life separate from her parents."

He didn't want to think of his mother *getting on* with anything. It was even more disturbing than his grandparents' bedroom affairs. "I still don't think it's a good idea. Is that what prompted the change in hairstyle?"

"Yes. One of the tourists is doing my hair for the wedding tomorrow. She suggested the cut and your mother went for it. But Demetri, wait a few days before you talk to her about trying to find your father. This is the first spark of hope she's had in years, and she hasn't told her parents. She's going to wait until after the wedding to break the news."

"My grandfather won't be happy."

"Then we better get him a big supply of blue pills."

"Rania."

"All right. I had no idea you were a prude, Demetri Christodoulou."

"I'm not a prude. I simply believe some things are better left private. Other things, however, need to be discussed. What's this about sleeping pills and some scheme you've undoubtedly talked my mother and grandmother into?"

Rania heaved a sigh. "Every year *Yiayia* wants to enter her vegetables into the island harvest contest. Then the week before the festival, someone creeps into her garden at night and cuts into the best ones so they are ruined. Two nights ago, we set up a little trap. We strung a wire between two batteries, making a temporary electric fence. The culprit burned his hands but we don't think it will stop him. She's going to pick the vegetables tomorrow, so tonight's the last night we have to keep guard."

"I can't believe you did that." His mind flashed to Kosta's bandaged hands. According to his grandmother, Kosta had won every year for the past ten years. It didn't surprise Demetri that he'd done it by using dirty tricks. "Where do the sleeping tablets come in?"

"Your grandfather almost caught us last time, and *Yiayia* doesn't think he'll approve of our methods, especially as the culprit is his best friend. So we thought we'd slip a little sleeping pill in with his dinner. Then he'll wake tomorrow refreshed and none-the-wiser. They're harmless over-the-counter pills. I use them all the time when I travel."

"And if I forbid you to carry out this plan?"

She crossed her arms over her chest, which drew his eyes to her breasts. Tomorrow couldn't come soon enough, provided she didn't get herself caught and arrested for her meddling. Kosta's son was the island's police officer.

"If you forbid it, then of course I'll listen to you, Demetri." She batted her eyelashes and looked like she'd never had a naughty thought in her life. If he tried to stop her, he had a feeling he'd wake up on his grandparents' sofa with a sleeping pill hangover. It would be better if he went with her and kept her out of trouble.

"I'm coming with you."

"Great, we need someone strong to carry the ammo."

• • •

Rania tried to subtly shift her body away from Demetri's, a near impossibility as the hiding place behind the compost pile barely hid her, never mind Demetri's big body. It was hard to concentrate when every nerve tingled and her senses were on high alert for the brush of his hand on her skin.

"This is not how I imagined spending my last night as a single man," Demetri whispered in her ear.

"One of the tourists in the nudist colony is an exotic dancer. I'm sure she'd give you a more traditional stag night. The woman is a genius with a glue gun. Want me to call her for you?"

"I don't even want to know anymore. And I'd better stay here, otherwise I'll be left standing at the altar while my bride sits in the storage room of the café, which doubles as a jail on this island."

"Don't worry, your mother has a key to the storage room. She'll spring me in time for the wedding."

"Rania."

Her whole body shook with silent laughter until he pushed her over so she was flat on her back on the hard ground, Demetri on top of her. His mouth covered her outraged gasp and within a minute she couldn't remember why she was outside lying in the dirt. She managed to free one hand trapped between them and ran it up and down his back under his T-shirt.

He shifted his body slightly and cupped her breast, his thumb rubbing over her nipple until it went hard. As his hand shifted down her body she moaned a protest at the loss of his touch. He slid his hand under the hem of her shirt and had just touched the bare skin of her stomach when a loud curse in Greek broke through to the tiny part of her brain not consumed with lust. Demetri must have heard it, too, because he stilled and then rolled off her.

"Watch out for an electrified wire," the gruff voice of Kosta came clearly through the dark.

Rania sat up and handed Demetri a pair of night vision goggles and they watched as Kosta and two of his sons carefully searched the ground for the batteries Rania had set up two nights ago.

First Rania concentrated on getting her body under control. If Kosta came closer, he'd hear her heavy breathing and be alerted to their presence. When she managed that, well, as best as she could as Demetri was still touching every inch of the left side of her body, she glanced over to where Maria and *Yiayia* were hiding. *Yiayia* gave the prearranged signal of rustling the leaves as though a mouse were scurrying away.

They waited until the three intruders were smack dab in the middle of the garden. Then Maria began taking photos, the flash from her camera blinding the intruders. Seconds later, the air was full of flying missiles as Rania and *Yiayia* used slingshots to hurl small potatoes, green tomatoes, and other sundry vegetables at the trio. A shot from *Yiayia* hit Kosta directly in the crotch with a large potato. The man screamed before doubling over with the pain. His two sons ran, leaving their father behind.

"If you ever come near my vegetables again, Kosta Kalvinou, I will make sure you don't walk upright for the rest of your life. Now get out of my garden!" *Yiayia* yelled in Greek.

Kosta struggled to his feet before limping away. All the while Maria was taking pictures, the camera's flash following him like a hail of light bullets. As he disappeared into the night, Maria climbed down from her perch in a pine tree.

Yiayia let out a yelp of triumph before hugging her daughter. The two women went over to where Rania and Demetri were still crouched behind the compost pile.

"We did it!" Maria said, her face alive with excitement. "I'm so tempted to put these photos up on Facebook, then the whole island will know what a sniveling cheat Kosta is. And how cowardly his two sons are leaving their father wounded in the field of battle."

"Keep the photos. They may come in handy later," *Yiayia* said.

It seemed Demetri had learned the art of blackmail from his grandmother.

"And you were no help." Maria rounded on her son. "Distracting our leader at the most crucial time."

"What do you mean?" Demetri's attempt at an innocent expression was ruined when he bent down and kissed Rania's neck.

"I was up the tree, remember. I could see everything. If I hadn't dropped the pine cone on Kosta's head, you would have missed the whole thing."

"Next time you stay home, Demetri," *Yiayia* said.

"Next time? There will be no next time," Demetri replied.

Rania turned in his arms and looked up at him. "Of course not, *habibi*. Our work here is done." Then she turned around again. "Ma, can you remind me to get a large supply of sleeping pills next time I'm off the island."

Demetri groaned.

Yiayia laughed like a schoolgirl. "We should get matching outfits," she said. "Then we can sort out all sorts of problems on this island." She blew across the top of her slingshot as if it were a smoking gun before holstering it in her apron pocket.

"After tomorrow, Rania is going to be far too busy to engage in vigilante activities." To prove his point, Demetri kissed her again.

"All right," his mother said. "We get the picture. It's after midnight, Demetri. You aren't supposed to see the bride on the wedding day until she comes to the church. Off you go."

Maria stood on tiptoe and gave her son a kiss on the cheek.

"I need to take Rania home."

"She's sleeping at our place tonight."

Rania could see the disappointment on his face that they weren't going to have a private moment before the wedding.

He walked with them back to his grandparents' house and after a kiss on the cheeks of all three women, he waved goodbye.

Rania watched until the taillights of the Jeep disappeared over the hill. Tomorrow she was going to marry the man. It may be the stupidest thing she'd ever done, but at the moment it felt so right, which meant it was bound to end in disaster.

· · ·

Rania stared at herself in the full-length mirror, trying to marshal a smile on her face. *Yiayia* and Maria were in tears. Rania wanted to cry, too, but for a different reason. The dress was so not her. Of course, as it was *Yiayia's* she couldn't really say anything. Demetri's grandmother had asked if Rania would wear her wedding dress. How could she say no to the older lady?

It had been a fashionable dress on the more slender bride fifty years ago. Even though they'd let out the seams at the bust and through the hips, Rania looked like she'd been shoved into it none-too-elegantly. And it was foot to neck with lace and had long lace sleeves. She was a fraud. Who gets married knowing it will only last a year?

Marriage may not have been high on Rania's to-do list, but she had expected one day to hitch herself to some stud. And, as with most women, she'd thought about her wedding day, especially when her sisters married. Rania had mentally chosen the type of wedding gown she'd buy—off the shoulder, fitted to the hips to show her curves, then flaring out in folds of silk. Not a hint of lace, and definitely no sleeves. This was so not her dream wedding.

For the past week she'd kept herself so busy she hadn't had time to think about what she was doing, and with Demetri away it had been easy to forget that in an hour she was going to pledge her life to the man. Well, a year of her life anyway. Now, staring in the mirror, wearing a white gown, with two weeping women behind her, it was all too real.

She could still run away. She could make up some excuse to go up to the pink house and then sneak down the other side of the hill and bribe a fisherman to take her off the island, except she knew she wouldn't do any of those things. Demetri's family seemed to need her almost as much as her uncle. If she left now, they'd probably go back to the way they were before—no one saying anything, everyone too afraid of failure to try something new.

Her phone pinged with an incoming text message and she grabbed it like a lifeline in a raging storm.

Demetri: *Don't even think of running away. I will follow you forever.*

Was it a threat or some sort of declaration that he would never let her go? Well, the Demetri equivalent of never being a year. Her fingers hesitated over the keys. It was a bit disconcerting that he'd text her at the very moment she was thinking of leaving.

Rania: *Don't worry. I think your grandmother will Taser me if I try to escape.*

Demetri: *Yiayia has a Taser? Where did she get a Taser?*

Rania: *Umm…*

"Everything all right, Rania?" Maria was still dabbing at her eyes with a tissue as she asked.

"Yes, everything is fine. Demetri was making sure I didn't have cold feet," Rania replied.

"You two are made for each other. He's too serious and you're too adventurous. Together you make a perfect couple. I couldn't be happier that you are my daughter."

Rania tried to swallow the lump in her throat. Maybe she should call off the wedding. It would be better to hurt these wonderful people a little bit now than a whole hell of a lot later on. She clutched the phone tighter in her hand. Could she?

"Are you ladies ready? It is time to go," *Pappous* said from the other side of the door.

"We're ready," *Yiayia* replied, opening the door.

Pappous's eyes were suspiciously bright as he looked at Rania. Whether he was remembering his own wedding day or lamenting the fact that he'd never seen his daughter get married, she didn't know.

She pushed all the questions, doubts, and fears to the back of her mind. Time to do this, Rania style.

"I'm ready," she said with more confidence than she felt. The ten-minute drive to the small church took twenty as every other person on the island was also making their way there. With little parking, cars were scattered all over the side of the road. Finally, three hundred meters from the church, the road was completely blocked.

I can't believe I have to walk to my own wedding.

She weaved her way between cars, clutching the flowers and herbs from *Yiayia's* garden while trying to prevent the dress from dragging on the dirt road. If her sisters could see her now, they'd be in fits of laughter. Her eldest sister had arrived at her wedding in a white Rolls Royce, her second sister in a horse-drawn carriage.

As Rania neared the church, she spotted Demetri standing on the steps, next to the priest. Was he ready to chase her down if she chickened out at the last minute?

Maria stopped her with a hand on her arm. "The ceremony starts outside, with the priest blessing the rings. He'll then lead you and Demetri into the church."

After a last fussing about with her hair and dress Maria and *Yiayia* stepped back and left her to face her future husband and the man who would bind them together.

Run, run her mind chanted. *You can't go through with this. You can't marry a man you don't love and barely know.* Then Uncle Fouad's gentle, encouraging voice filled her mind. "You can do anything, Rania. You are the most determined person I know."

"For Uncle Fouad," she said under her breath, hoping the auditory reassurance would stop her knees from shaking.

Demetri's gaze met hers and as if in a trance, Rania started to walk toward him. As she glided nearer, she saw the challenge in his eyes. Rania Ghalli didn't back down from a challenge. She'd wed this man, then make him rue the day he ever blackmailed her into marriage. She'd turn his life upside down, and when she left, he'd wonder how he was ever going to live without her.

They exchanged rings three times on the steps, then followed the priest into the church. Rania half listened to the melodious chanting in Greek. She smiled and nodded, bowed her head and stood still as *Pappous*, acting as the *Koumbaro*, three times exchanged the crowns the priest placed on her and Demetri's heads. When at last the ceremony was done, her new husband leaned down and pressed a gentle kiss on her lips.

"My wife," he whispered.

She looked out over the assembled crowd. The church was packed with people standing at the sides and back, and not a single person she'd met before last week. Definitely not her dream wedding.

Demetri took her hand and led her out of the church and down the street to the café where Maria used to work. A couple of marquis tents had been set up at the back to accommodate the overflow of guests. They circled among the crowd. Rania introduced Demetri to as many people as he did her. All the tourists who had helped with the house were there, including her Viagra supplying plumber.

She did her best to join in the party, but her heart wasn't in it. Several men were performing traditional Greek dances. Demetri had joined them until a couple of minutes ago when he'd come to stand beside her, his arm around her waist. The dress itched wherever the lace touched her bare skin, and if she ate another bite, she was sure half the buttons would ping from her back like pearl-shaped shrapnel.

A smile twerked her lips upward and Demetri whispered into her ear. "At last, a smile. Are you okay?"

"Yeah. It's just…well…not the day I imagined. Even scheming bitches dream of their wedding day."

"What about the wedding night?" His lips brushed the centimeter of bare skin between the ruffled lace collar of the dress and her ear.

"We spare a passing thought for it." Damn the breathiness in her voice.

"I'll make sure that, at least, doesn't disappoint you." Demetri took her hand and strode over to his mother and *Yiayia. Pappous* was dancing like a man half his age, slapping the floor and kicking his legs in the air. "Thank you for all the arrangements and for making our wedding day special. Rania and I are going to leave now. I hope you can get *Pappous* off the dance floor before dawn, and that he doesn't injure himself." He kissed his mother and grandmother on their cheeks.

There were rounds of hugging, and once word of their imminent departure spread it took almost another hour before they finally stood outside the café. A cool breeze was welcome on her lace-covered itchy skin. Cars were still haphazardly parked in the town's main road.

"Looks as though we may have to walk home," she said.

"Be right back."

Demetri returned a minute later with a small key in hand. He led her over to a decrepit motorbike, which was leaning against the patio railing. Her sisters would laugh themselves silly if they heard she'd left her wedding reception on the back of an old motorbike. At least it was better than walking. She climbed on sidesaddle behind her new husband and held on for dear life. It took every ounce of her concentration to stay on over the rough terrain and keep *Yiayia's* dress out of the back wheel. Finally, they arrived at the pink house.

Standing under the ink black sky, dotted with millions of stars, every cell in her body was aware of Demetri next to her. As she tried to fit the key into the lock her hand was shaking so much he took the key from her. What was the problem? She'd had sex before. But this was sex with Demetri, and she was pretty sure it would be a whole new experience.

Let the adventure begin.

Chapter Eight

Demetri dragged in a lungful of the fresh night air as he took the key from Rania. He hadn't even kissed her yet and already he felt intoxicated. She was his wife — at last. The thought sent a quiver through him. It was as though he'd been waiting for her forever. Two weeks ago he didn't even know she existed. Hopefully once they'd made love he could get back on an even keel and concentrate on business and building his empire. With a little added spice while Rania was around.

Why was she so nervous? She'd flirted with him and kissed him like an experienced lover. She couldn't be...

"Rania, this isn't your first time, is it?" Every muscle tensed. Although which answer he was hoping for he wasn't sure. To be her first and know that no man had ever tasted her before was a heady thought. Yet to initiate her in the ways of love would require a lot of patience, a virtue he definitely lacked whenever he looked at her.

"First time getting married? Yup."

"First time making love."

"I think you mean marital-sanctified copulation."

He smiled but didn't laugh. "Rania, are you a virgin?"

"No. I've had sex before." She shuffled a pebble off the path and into the flowerbed with her shoe.

"But not like this." He raised her face to his as she tried to hide her expression in the dark.

"No. It seems different somehow. Less spontaneous. More permanent."

He wished she hadn't said that word. The entire day, through the whole elaborate Orthodox ceremony, he'd continually reminded himself this was only a temporary arrangement, a needed step to secure the property. He'd tried to focus on the land. Too bad all this attention was on the woman next to him. For tonight at least.

"Show me what you've done to this shack, aside from paint it pink." He unlocked the door. *Should I carry her across the threshold?* Before he could decide, she barreled into the room.

He stepped in slowly behind her, amazed at the change to the place in the week he'd been gone. It was still tiny, but now cozy. A slate floor had been laid and a stack of huge, colorful cushions rested against a newly plastered but unpainted wall. The small kitchen had been completely remodeled with new and compact appliances. Well-worn wood counter tops and mismatched crockery made it look like it had been used for years.

In the sink sat a bottle of French champagne; a few ice cubes still floated in the water. Two gold-rimmed champagne flutes were next to it on the counter. A note was propped against the glasses. *Singariteeria, Christina.*

Rania flicked the card between her fingers. "Not every day the ex-girlfriend congratulates a former lover on his marriage."

"Christina and I were never lovers."

"Well, don't expect me to send you champagne when you

remarry."

"No. I would never expect that of you." He uncorked the sparkling wine and poured two glasses, handing one to his bride.

"What do you expect of me, Demetri?" She raised her head and speared him through the heart with her amber eyes.

"Honesty. Trust. Loyalty."

"Those things have to be earned."

"I'll earn them, but I must have a down-payment. Be honest with me and I'll reciprocate. Trust me to get your uncle out of prison. And never hurt my family. That's all."

She finished the champagne he'd given her then refilled the flute. A few bubbles escaped the rim of the glass. With a deft finger she scooped them up and placed them on her lips. He was mesmerized as her tongue swept out and captured the bubbles. Heat flooded his groin. As if sensing his discomfort, a mischievous smile creased her lips. She stepped closer and ran a finger from his bottom lip, down his chin to the open neck of his shirt. "Really? Is that all you want, *azizy*?" The husky timber of her voice sent the rest of his blood south, leaving his heart to beat empty.

"No, that's not all. I think it's time you showed me the bedroom."

"Grab the champagne," she said before opening a door at the other end of the room.

He pulled the bottle out of the sink, not caring that water dripped down onto his thousand-euro suit. With the heat emanating from him, it would soon turn to steam and evaporate anyway.

Demetri stepped into the room and stopped. Whatever he'd been expecting, it wasn't this. He was glad he'd brought her back to the house and not the boat. This room was made for sexy times. The walls and ceiling were covered in multi-colored fabrics—hues of blue, gold, red, and purple. An ornate chandelier somehow hung in the middle, sending shards of light throughout the room, creating interesting shadows and areas of intense color. The floor was covered in a variety of rugs, some new, some old. The room was sensuous, exotic, Rania.

When he finally pulled his gaze from the decor, Rania stood at the end of the bed, sipping her champagne. She'd pulled the pins from her hair, and it now fell around her shoulders and down her back in wild abandon. He drank his champagne to ease the dryness in his throat. After refilling Rania's glass and his own, he put the bottle down on a table by the door.

"This room is amazing."

"My mother is from a Bedouin tribe. It was quite a scandal when she married my father. Eventually, her family accepted my dad. And when my father was on an archeological dig, we often lived with them in tents nearby. It's an interesting life, and I think I've inherited the nomadic tendencies. I've found it hard to settle since we left Egypt."

"I'm looking forward to getting to know all about you and your interesting family. But later." He took her empty champagne glass and put it with his next to the bottle, then he returned to stand in front of her. Her chest heaved as she took in a deep breath.

"I have a challenge for you," she said as he lowered his head to kiss her.

He tasted her lips; the champagne had cooled her mouth, but soon it was hot as their tongues dueled. She raised her arms and put one in his hair while the other roamed his back, pulling him closer. He should have taken off his jacket when he'd removed his tie earlier. Hell, he should have taken off all his clothes while she talked.

"What's this challenge?" He let her go long enough to pull the jacket off and toss it across the room.

"There are 101 buttons on this dress. You have to undo every single one of them to get me out of it. Trust me, I know. I challenge you to undo them all, carefully. If even one falls off, you lose."

"Interesting. What do I get when I win?"

"Me."

"A worthy prize. What happens if I lose? If I rip the dress from your body and not a single button remains?"

She sucked in another deep breath. Her breasts strained against the material covering them. The second option definitely seemed the better one. And even if he lost, he was pretty sure she wouldn't deny him.

"Then you have to explain to your *yiayia* what happened to her dress. Tell her that you were too impatient a lover to take the time to properly undress your bride."

Not a conversation he wanted to have. "I accept your challenge. However, if you rip the dress or pop a button, then you have to tell *yiayia* it was you who was too impatient."

She swallowed again. "You're on."

He almost rubbed his hands in glee as his grandmother had done last night. *I'll have her begging me to take her before even half of them are undone.*

"Turn around," he said, his voice strained as he struggled for a semblance of control.

He released the first ten tiny pearl buttons, kissing her back as each centimeter of skin was exposed. He never knew a spine could be so sexy. Maybe it was the tremble in Rania each time his lips touched her. After five glorious minutes, he'd reached the middle of her back. Just enough. He gently eased the dress off her shoulders, trapping her arms by her side. With ten buttons on each sleeve holding the fabric tight to her forearms, she couldn't take her arms out either.

Demetri moved in front of Rania, resting against the high footboard of the bed. He placed her between his outstretched legs, then flicked the front opening of her bra. Her breasts spilled from their restraints as if happy to be free at last, not as happy as he was to see them unbound. His dick jerked simply looking at the bounty before him.

At first he stared and her nipples puckered under his gaze. Rania hauled in one deep breath after another. "Demetri," she moaned as he finally reached out to touch her. He took his time fondling, caressing, and trailing his fingers from the top to the bottom, making leisurely circles around her tight nipples. When he took the right nipple in his mouth and flicked it with his tongue a low moan of longing escaped her, fueling his desire.

He clamped down on his own raging need. Rania had challenged him. Demetri Christodoulou would win, as always. By the time he was finished, for now, with her breasts, she was breathing so heavily he worried she may pass out. "Easy now, *agape mou*. We're less than halfway done with the buttons. Careful you don't pop any."

"I should have challenged you to see how fast you could get me out of this dress."

"Too late to change the rules now." He moved over to the small table and grabbed the champagne bottle. Pouring a tiny amount into his palm, he then washed her breasts with the bubbly liquid, careful not to get any on the dress.

"Are you going to lick it off?" Rania asked as he put the bottle on the floor and then moved to stand behind her again.

"Later. Keep your breasts up so it doesn't drip on the dress, or you'll have to explain the champagne stains on the inside to *Yiayia*."

She moaned again then thrust her chest out and forward, away from the dress. The buttons in the middle of her back strained but stood firm. He started at the bottom this time, under the curve of her ass. The dress must have been uncomfortable to sit in; no wonder she'd stood for most of the reception. With the closing so far down, it allowed him to fondle her as he slowly released each pearl from its loop. When he'd managed to get twenty buttons undone, he slipped his hand into the dress and between her thighs. The tiny lace thong was no barrier to his probing fingers. She was so hot and wet, he had to clench his teeth together to stop from ripping the rest of the dress off her right then and there.

She trembled against his hand as he stroked her; her legs shook so much he put his other arm around her waist to keep her upright.

"Demetri, please." His name escaped her lips as she hovered near the brink. He wanted to watch her come, see the passion on her face as she lost control. She moaned again as he removed his hand and stood in front of her. A tiny drop of champagne perched on the tip of her nipple, still thrust in the air. He quickly worked his hand under the front of her dress and continued to play with her most sensitive spot. With his tongue he touched the champagne before taking her nipple into his mouth, sucking hard.

With a strangled cry, Rania shattered. Her inner muscles clenched around his fingers. Her lower body shook so much he had to concentrate to keep his thumb on the center of her passion. Her face was beautiful. Desire was etched in every curve; a deep flush turned her tanned skin darker. Her lips parted as she sucked in lungsful of air like a woman rescued from the sea.

He slid his hands from her warmth as he kissed her long and hard. "We've reached the halfway point now," he whispered against her lips.

"Oh God."

"Told you I didn't need instructions. Although I will say your breasts are full and very tasty." She laughed and it was nearly his undoing. Blind lust overcame him.

"Get me out of this dress." She probably meant to sound

commanding. The breathiness of her voice made it sexy.

"As you wish, wife."

He returned to her back, slowly slipping one button after another through the delicate loop. With each one released he'd kiss the skin on her back and run a finger from the top down or bottom up. When the last one was undone, he again returned to the front. The dress hung from her arms, a puddle of white silk and lace.

Demetri took her right hand in his, circling the palm with his tongue, then trailing tiny bites up her arm as he undid the buttons to her elbow. He repeated the caress with her left hand until the final button was vanquished.

"101 buttons, all accounted for. Now let's see my prize." He leaned back against the footboard as though examining a painting he was considering buying.

Rania let the dress fall along with her bra, then kicked it aside. She stood before him in white high-heels and the tiny thong that was still shoved to one side. Rania was so beautiful, her face still flushed from her orgasm, her chest heaving with each breath, that he was the one in danger of passing out.

"As you did such a good job undressing me, I shall have to see if I can meet your standards. Stand up, Demetri. It's my turn."

He swallowed. This might kill him.

• • •

Rania slowly circled her husband, considering the best line of attack. With no heating in the house, the air was frigid but she barely noticed it on her overheated skin. Demetri had serious lover skills. This year of captivity was going to fly by, but she wouldn't be bested by any man—even her husband. It was time he got a taste of his own medicine.

"My game now. New rules. You can't touch me, and if

your knees buckle, I win."

"What do you win?"

"I get to go on top for the next round."

"I don't see how I lose then."

"It's a mental victory."

"And if I win? If I remain standing no matter what you do to me?" He sounded confident but the hand he ran through his hair shook slightly.

"Then I'll bathe you tomorrow morning."

"Hmm, that sounds good, too."

"Excellent. Would you like a drink before we start?"

"No. I don't want anything to dull my senses. Bring it, Rania. Make me melt."

Oh, you'll melt all right. You are going down on your knees, Demetri Christodoulou.

"You don't mind if I have a little drink?"

Without waiting for his reply, she retrieved the champagne bottle. There was only a little bit left so she took a sip straight from the bottle then tipped the rest down her body, making sure to spread some over her breasts. Demetri's hot gaze fastened on her dark nipples and his tongue moistened his lips. She fondled her breasts then trailed a finger down her body to the top of her lace thong.

Demetri's breathing got heavier and his voice was strained. "Rania."

"Oh sorry. I was supposed to be undressing you, wasn't I? Hmm, where to start?" She circled him again, trailing a finger along his shoulders. When she reached the front, she slid a couple of buttons free on his shirt. Slipping her hands inside, she grazed his nipples with her fingers. Anxious to get her tongue on them, as he'd done to her, she quickly undid a few more buttons before shoving the shirt off his shoulders, trapping his arms as he had done to her.

She treated his chest to the same attention he'd given hers.

Heat spiraled once again between her legs and the tingling at the back of her thighs made standing in the stiletto heels difficult, but she was determined to make him beg.

Sliding her hands down his chest, she undid the buckle of his belt and the top button of his pants. She was immediately greeted with his erection pressing against her hand. "It appears someone wants to come out to play," she whispered against his lips.

"Very much so," Demetri said.

Torturously, she lowered his zipper, millimeter by millimeter. She continued to kiss him, her breasts lightly grazing his chest as she held her body far enough away to tantalize. His hands were bunched into fists at his side and a muscle throbbed in his jaw, not as much as the throbbing elsewhere. His pants finally undone, she shoved them from his hips to pool at his ankles. He kicked them off and they landed next to her wedding gown.

Rania stepped back to admire her work. His black boxers were straining to withhold his erection. His shirt was half off, his eyes heavily lidded as he stared at her. She reached out and ran a finger along his cock, which leapt at her touch. Demetri sucked in a breath between his teeth.

She made quick work of the rest of his clothes so that he stood naked in front of her. A magnificent male specimen. "There. Now I know what I have to work with."

Rania slipped off her shoes and handed them to Demetri before she knelt before him. Thank goodness she'd had the rugs put down. Still, she was too low so she grabbed a couple of large cushions from the corner and set to work exploring his lower half with her tongue and hands.

She licked his length, her tongue playing with him. When she glanced at his face, his jaw was clenched; his hands were holding her shoes so tight she thought the heels would snap off in his hands. His knees locked in place. He was fighting for control with all he had. "Everything okay up there?"

"Yes, all good."

"Excellent. Easy now, *azizy*, we're almost halfway done."

She continued exploring him, tasting, sucking, nipping with her teeth until she felt his legs begin to shake. Taking him into her mouth, she sucked hard until he grabbed her by the hair disengaging her mouth from him. He sank to his knees.

"You win. Bed, wall, floor, your choice. I have to be inside you. Now."

She rose to her feet, grabbed his hand, and led him over to the bed. Pushing on his chest, he tumbled onto the mattress, and she climbed on top.

"Wait. We need a condom," he said.

"I'm on the pill and healthy. For tonight I want nothing between us."

He nodded as if he couldn't form any more words. Their gazes locked as he slid into her and neither could hold back their moans of pleasure. She took a moment to enjoy the exquisite sensations coursing through her body before she began to move on him.

She'd expected the physical pleasure, although that had far surpassed her wildest fantasy. The emotional connection was a surprise she hadn't prepared for. This was more than marital-sanctified copulation. More than sex. More than the release of mutual desire. She'd found home. She tried to shut her mind to the thought, tried to distance herself from the discovery that her sanctuary was a man who only wanted her for a year; tried not to feel an overwhelming sense of completeness, knowing it couldn't last.

"Rania." Demetri said her name as though it was the only word he could form.

She pushed aside thoughts of the end and concentrated on the here and now. If only she could make this last forever, but control was impossible and pleasure exploded into a million fragments. Demetri's shout when he climaxed probably scared the local goat herd onto the next hill.

Satiated, she collapsed on top of him. "You promised me amazing and you delivered," she said when finally she could think in English.

"You haven't seen anything yet. Give me a couple minutes to recover, and I'll show you."

"You think you can top that?" It had been the best sex of her life. She wasn't sure if she could take much more.

"I know I can top it. I promise next time you'll be screaming my name."

"All right, Demetri. Make me scream your name, and I'll give you that bath."

Three hours later her voice was gone from screaming her pleasure. She couldn't move even if the zombie apocalypse began. Demetri had the biggest, most self-satisfied grin on his face, not that he'd been in complete control the whole time. He'd begged her on more than one occasion to keep doing what she was doing. As Rania lay on top of her husband, his hands ran down her back, over her bottom, and back up again.

"You've started calling me *azizy*. What does it mean?" His deep voice rumbled against her ear.

"It means my darling. I thought I'd upgrade you from *habibi* since we're married now."

"Hmm, I'm enjoying all the upgrades. This is shaping up to be the best year of my life." He pulled the sheet over her back and promptly fell asleep.

As his chest rose and fell with his deep breathing she wondered what would happen when their year was over. Would she be able to walk away unscathed? Or would Demetri ruin her for any other man? If Demetri became her home, where would she run when it was all over?

Chapter Nine

Demetri lay back in the cast iron tub and stared through the skylight at the patch of gray sky above his head. Last night had been a revelation, one he hadn't been prepared for. He'd expected the sex to be phenomenal but it had gone beyond physical enjoyment. He and Rania had connected on some other level—a level he hadn't even known existed. It was as though his soul was now fused with hers, which didn't bode well for an easy parting.

He forced his mind from thoughts of the future and focused on Rania's skills in home improvement. The more-than-functional bathroom had been added the week he'd been away. Tacked onto the bedroom, it had not only a very roomy shower but a full bath. Unfortunately, the water was heated by the sun through black coils on the roof. As it was rainy today, the water had been too cold to shower together. So they'd warmed water on the stove until the bath was the perfect temperature. Or it would be perfect if Rania were with him in the tub.

He could hear her in the bedroom, rummaging around for

something. "There it is," she said before appearing a moment later with two brown bottles in her hand. She wore a plain white dress that looked like it had been hastily made out of a bed sheet. Demetri bit back the disappointment that she'd put clothes on. Aside from an apron she'd worn while they made breakfast, the rest of the day had been spent in glorious nakedness. For the first time he appreciated the freedom the nudists who frequented the island experienced, except he wanted no other man to see Rania undressed. That pleasure was reserved for him alone.

Pleasure. That had reached a new definition with Rania as well. Was a year going to be enough?

She poured some of the liquid from the bottle onto a sponge and began to rub his back. He hadn't been bathed by a woman since he was five years old. An exotic scent filled the air and his skin tingled as every nerve ending stood at attention waiting for the next sensation.

"You haven't explained to me why our house is pink." He tried to force his mind off Rania's hands as they lathered him. She moved to the end of the bath, leaned over, and put his ankle on her shoulder. The water from his foot dripped onto her; a ribbon of water snaked down to her breast, soaking the material. The white dress became translucent, revealing tantalizing glimpses of her nipple. His mouth went dry.

"We plastered the outside of the house and most of the inside, but then ran out of material before we finished the bedroom. I worried that moisture would seep through and make the room feel damp. So the plasterer suggested painting the outside to stop any water getting through. The only color in enough quantity to do the job was pink. Someone ordered it by mistake, getting freesia and fuchsia confused. I did ask if you had any objections."

When she'd texted him asking if he minded the color fuchsia, he'd assumed she was referring to decorations for the wedding, not the outside color of his house. However, when she swept the sponge up his inner thigh, his mind went blank. "No, no objections."

As she placed his leg back in the water and reached for the other one, her breasts grazed the water. The whole top of her dress now clung to her. It was the most seductive thing he'd ever seen. A private wet-shirt contest. His body went hard. While she washed his leg, he lifted the other from the water and circled her nipples with his big toe. It was her turn to suck in a breath.

"You're not going to get washed doing that."

"I want to be dirty."

"I'm not putting my mouth on you unless you're clean."

He rose from the bath with such speed that half the water splashed out and Rania was soaked to her waist. As she lathered him, replacing the sponge with her hands, he stood stoically under her ministrations. Rania ripped him inside out with just a touch, reduced his control to ashes, and destroyed his will to do anything except make love to her. He was a captive, and it didn't sit well with him. But he'd promised himself twenty-four hours. After that it was back to business. Until then...

"Rania," he gasped out as she took him in her mouth. "No more games. We do this together this time. Take off your dress."

She released him and stood. With him still standing in the bath, she appeared tiny before him. "Rip it from me." What did they say about dynamite and small packages?

He paused. He'd never ripped a woman's clothes off before. It smacked of barbarianism and a lack of civility. Then again, he'd never been so tempted before.

Rania ran her hands up his body, pulled his head down, and kissed him. The need to have her naked against him was overwhelming, and he grabbed the neckline of her dress and ripped it clear to the hem. He could feel her smile against his lips.

"You enjoy it when I lose control, don't you?"

She shrugged off the shoulders of the ruined dress, letting it drop into the puddle of water on the pebble tiled floor. "You're not losing control. You're being real. Dropping all the pretenses and bullshit you put up between yourself and those around you. When we make love, you hold nothing back. That's the man I want standing beside me, the one not ashamed of who he is, pretending to be someone else."

She'd seen through his façade, seen through the controlled persona he used to hide his insecurities. She'd not seen the wealthy businessman who'd built a successful empire. She'd seen him. And, it appeared, liked that man better than the one he pretended to be so others didn't figure out who he really was.

After all he'd accomplished, it shouldn't matter that he was a bastard, considered inferior by his grandfather. But to him it still did. The truth of her words stung. "I'm not ashamed." He dropped his hands from her and stepped out of the bath. She was tiny. In her bare feet her head barely reached his shoulder.

"Good. Then you can stop trying to prove you're worthy of being a Christodoulou to your grandfather and get on with living your own life."

Another direct hit. "I'm not discussing this with you. You've known him for one week and you have the nerve to lecture me on my relationship with my *pappous*?"

"Sometimes it takes an outsider to see how things really are."

"Things are fine the way they are." He crossed his arms and dared her to challenge him again.

Rania put a hand on his face, caressing his cheek with her thumb. "You forget, Demetri, I'm a Christodoulou now, too.

Your family is my family. Your problems my problems. We're in this together."

"For one year only, or less if we both get what we want before then."

She dropped her hand and leaped back as though he'd struck her physically. "How stupid of me to forget. I'd better get on with my wifely duties while there's still time. I'll start dinner." Spinning on her heel, she left the bathroom, her head high, her gorgeous ass swaying beneath her wealth of hair. Even angry he was turned on. Damn the woman, but she got under his skin. Tomorrow he'd start negotiations to buy the land, then they'd leave Gavdos. Away from his family, she wouldn't be able to interfere, and he'd be able to prove to her exactly what type of man he was—wealthy and in control.

• • •

Rania stirred the couscous in the pot before removing it from the heat. With only one burner and a fridge the size of a small cooler, cooking was more innovation than creation. But she didn't figure they'd be staying long on the island. She'd just overheard Demetri on the phone saying he wanted to meet with someone before they left tomorrow afternoon. At least she assumed she was going with him this time. If he left her alone again…well, she wouldn't be here when he returned.

"Need a hand?"

She jumped at his deep voice right behind her.

"No, I've got it. There's no room in here for both of us anyway." And with his hot body pressed against hers it was hard not to forget the food and do him on the kitchen table. If she wasn't careful, she'd become his love slave doing anything, becoming anything, just for a caress and a kiss.

"Are you sure?"

I'm not sure about anything anymore.

"Yes. Five minutes then it will be ready. I think there's a bottle of wine in one of the bags by the front window. Why don't you open it while I plate up?"

She heard him rummage through a couple of gift bags. "What is all this stuff?"

"Wedding presents. I told everyone we didn't need anything. A few insisted on giving us something. I thought maybe we could store them in your house in Crete and then when we split up, we can return the gifts. I'm sure they won't miss a bottle of wine, though, or we can replace it with one from your cellar." She was babbling now, but it was better than the chilled silence of the previous half hour.

Before she could even turn over the lamb kebobs, Demetri was standing next to her again. He handed her a glass of wine and then he swirled the dark red liquid in his glass. "Fifty percent of marriages end in divorce these days. I'm sure those people don't give back their wedding presents."

"And I'm sure those people didn't go into their marriage knowing it wasn't going to last. What we've done is wrong on so many levels. It's going to devastate your mother when we split."

He shrugged and continued to stare at his wine. "She'll get over it."

"Like she got over your father?"

He looked at her then, his eyes hard, his lips tight. "Rania."

"All right. I'll stay out of it." *Kind of, sort of. Well, I'll try.*

"Dinner smells amazing." Change of subject. "I'm going to put on ten kilos being married to you."

"Don't worry, *azizy*. I'll make sure you work off the calories."

Finally a smile. He bent down and kissed her cheek. "I'll hold you to that."

He'd hold her to a promise of sex. The vow she'd made to love and care for him was dispensable. No point worrying about the end already; there was still plenty of time to enjoy. She put her wine glass down and quickly plated the food. They ate at the table, all proper like. Brunch had been eaten on the cushions on the floor, Bedouin style. They'd fed each other until other hungers had taken over and they'd made love.

"So, what's the plan for the rest of the week, month, year?" She forced her mind to think practical, not sensual.

"Tomorrow morning I'm meeting with Christina's uncle who owns the land I want to buy. He was at the wedding so there should be no objections to my purchase. Then we leave for Crete. I have a few meetings next week on the island. And I also need to visit the resort where the murder happened, make sure it's ready to reopen and the staff have coped with the trauma."

"And me?"

"You'll come with me, of course."

She tilted her head and stared at him. Did he think she was some sort of dog to follow her master around?

"What if I choose to stay here?"

Demetri put down his fork and knife. "You're my wife. You belong at my side."

"I belong trying to get my uncle out of prison."

"I told you I had that in hand. You said you'd trust me." He folded his arms across his chest, abandoning his meal.

"Demetri, do you know how many people have told me the same thing? I waited three months while a man I was dating 'handled it.' All he did was write to his local Member of Parliament and send an email to the Egyptian President's office."

"I am not some man you're dating. I've already discovered what prison your uncle is in and we're making discreet inquiries as to the best way to free him. If you go barreling in with one of your half-thought-out plans, you'll jeopardize everything I've done."

"So I just have to trust you?"

"Yes."

"I—"

"Rania, I may not love you, but in everything else I intend to live up to my role as your husband. I will protect you, care for you, and see that your needs are met. That includes rescuing your uncle. When we get to Crete, I'll introduce you to my lawyer who is handling the negotiations. You can pester him for constant updates if you like."

"All right. Tell me about this land you're so desperate for you would marry a woman you don't love."

"I'm getting more from this marriage than the property." His hot gaze roved over her, setting off sparks of awareness across her skin. If tonight was anything like last night, she'd better eat up. She'd need the stamina.

Rania resumed eating. "So, the land you want is on Gavdos?"

"Yes, directly below my grandparents' house. The crescent bay."

"It's beautiful. It'll make a stunning location for a house, although the cost of building will be astronomical. Why bother when you don't plan to stay long on the island? Is it for your mother? Because I asked if she wanted to live in this place while we're away, and she said she doesn't want to be alone. Of course, if she gets together with your father, or some other man, then she'll need her own house."

Rania glanced up in time to see Demetri's jaw clench when she mentioned his mother's future. He was worse than an over-protective parent. If they ever had children, especially girls, he'd probably make them wear some kind of chastity belt. She quickly shut down the thought of bearing his children. Looked as if motherhood was also off her agenda, at least until she was over Demetri, by which time her eggs would probably have withered into nothing.

"I plan to build a resort there. So every time my grandfather sits on his porch my success will stare him in the face."

"A resort on Gavdos? Have you run a cost analysis? The return on investment is going to be abysmal, if it ever gets out of the red."

"How do you know?"

"I have a degree in environmental engineering and my uncle owns a construction business; I know the work involved. I've also been on the property. The slope is unstable, the gradient steep, access to fresh water limited. Putting a septic system with enough capacity to handle a small resort is going to cost a fortune. That plus the lack of basic infrastructure on the island with few historical sites or other lures to draw visitors means it's going to have to be spectacular to get even a consideration on the tourist sites. And how are you going to get clients here? In the week I've lived on the island the ferry has canceled twice. The people who are willing to pay what you're going to have to charge to just break even don't want any uncertainty about when they can come and go. You'll never get an investor to put their money in, given those factors."

"I don't plan on getting any outside investments. I'm going to fund it myself." Demetri resumed eating but didn't meet her gaze.

"You're going to risk your fortune to spit in your grandfather's face?"

"I knew you wouldn't understand."

"No, I don't understand. Rather than try to find some common ground with your grandfather—or heaven forbid, actually discuss the way you feel—you're more invested in proving him wrong, making the breach between you permanent."

"There's no relationship to fix, Rania. He hated me before I was born. Anything I do or don't do isn't going to change that. *Pappous* sent me away when I was twelve, hoping I'd never come back. Well, I am back, and I intend to leave a permanent reminder that he has a grandson, no matter how ashamed he is of me."

Demetri picked up his plate and put it in the kitchen sink. He stared out the back window into the pitch-black night. From his reflection in the glass, she could see his jaw clench and unclench.

His wounds were so deep that one week and a night of loving weren't going to heal them. Rania moved to stand behind her husband. She placed a hand on his back, between his shoulder blades. He tensed for a second then relaxed as she ran her hand over him. After massaging his shoulders for a couple of minutes, he turned and put her arms around his neck. His hands on her waist drew her against him.

"I don't believe your grandfather is ashamed of you. I think he's ashamed of himself. Your success highlights his failures. *Yiayia* told me he tried to start a business and lost everything. Please, Demetri. Please, give it a few months before you make any definite plans for the land." She pulled his head down to hers and kissed him tenderly.

"I make no promises, but I'll think about what you said."

"Good. In the meantime, if you do the dishes, I'll give you an all-over body massage with some special lotion."

"You're on."

• • •

Rania flicked a section of her long hair back over her shoulder. The chestnut waves beckoned his hands as always, luring him to bury his face in their softness, let the strands slip through his fingers as he ravished her mouth. Now wasn't the time to get distracted so he allowed himself only to lean closer and inhale deeply of her scent. Later, when this day was over and they retired to their private villa…

They were at his resort on Naxos where the murder had occurred two weeks ago. Today the first load of new visitors would arrive since the tragedy, and he wanted to be on hand to ease any tension on the part of the staff or guests. At least he had Rania here with him this time. Her warmth and compassion had already won over all of his staff. She'd hugged and spoken individually to each employee last night at the get together he'd arranged to make sure everyone was coping and ready to reopen.

The shuttle van from the airport drew up outside the reception area and Rania's hand around his waist squeezed him lightly. The smile she flashed him as he gazed down shot warmth all the way to his toes. When he'd been here right after the tragedy, he couldn't comprehend how a man could kill his wife rather than let her leave him. It was still incomprehensible to Demetri, but he could at least understand a little of the desperation the murderer must have felt.

Even though they'd gone into their marriage knowing it had a time limit, Demetri wasn't quite sure how he was going to let Rania go when they both had what they wanted. She'd brought even more to the marriage than sex and laughter. She supported and encouraged him as passionately as she made love, and she challenged him to see beyond the obvious and give others the benefit of the doubt. Rania made him a better man.

The first clients stepped through the sliding glass doors and into the reception. Rania approached and warmly greeted each one as they entered, as though welcoming invited guests into her home. If he'd just come off a charter flight and then endured a bumpy, hour-long transfer, a beautiful woman welcoming him personally was exactly what he'd want. If he were a tourist, he'd never want to leave. Or he'd return again and again. Rania was pure marketing genius.

A little girl, about three years old, cried loudly as her father set her on the floor while he searched for the family's passports. Rania grabbed something from behind the reception desk and hurried over to the child. She knelt next to the girl and presented her with a shiny plastic tiara. The toddler's tears turned into smiles, earning Rania effusive thanks from the exhausted parents. For a second, Demetri's mind flashed to an image of Rania consoling their child and his chest tightened. Babies were not part of the original deal.

The door swooshed open again and he forced his eyes from his wife to the newly arrived guest. *What the hell is she doing here?* He hurried over.

"Athena, welcome." He forced a smile on his face. "To what do we owe the pleasure of your company?" Pompous ass was back again, as Rania would say. Hearing his wife's voice in his head brought a genuine smile to his lips.

"I thought I'd show my support, after, well, you know…" The socialite's eyes scanned the reception area dismissively before settling warmly on him. A month ago he'd have considered the invitation in her eyes; now it made his skin crawl.

"Are we expecting you? I didn't see your name on the registered guest list." A uniformed chauffeur was piling bags in the corner, six at the last count.

"I didn't think you'd be too busy. Surely the Alexander suite is available." That she knew the name of his most expensive accommodation was a slight surprise. Her father owned a rival resort business in Greece. Although rather than aim at the family-friendly market where Demetri was carving out a niche, Athena's father's resorts were aimed at the twenty-somethings wanting to party. Hedonism was the theme of their resorts. Demetri had considered an alliance with them, and he'd even dated Athena a few times, but he'd found her acidic personality difficult to stomach. She found fault with everything and everyone.

"I'm afraid my wife and I are staying in the Alexander suite. I'll check to see what else we have available that would suit you."

He strode over to the reception desk and snagged a spare computer. They'd offered a substantial discount on their regular rates to valued customers to get the resort full this late in the season. The only suite they had left was where the murder occurred. It had been completely cleaned and Athena probably wouldn't object. In fact, from what he knew of her, she'd probably enjoy sleeping where some other poor woman lost her life in a crime of passion. But could he ask his staff to service the room daily so soon?

Glancing up from the screen, he saw Rania approach Athena. The two women stood next to each other and Demetri couldn't help running a comparison analysis. Both were beautiful, in different ways. Athena was tall and willowy with wealth dripping from every pore. Her clothes, jewelry, and attitude all screamed money. Athena's luggage alone was worth more than a month in the Alexander suite.

Rania was shorter, curvier, and had on a simple cotton sundress and wore only the rings he'd given her. But the difference in their two personalities was like comparing a bottle of vinegar to a rich, full-bodied red wine. His wife intoxicated him with just a look.

He strode over to the women. "I'm sorry, Athena. We're booked full," he said.

"Surely you can find something for a friend, Demi." She pouted, obviously unused to being denied. "The Alexander suite has two rooms. Maybe I can share with you?"

Rania's gaze shot to his, a flash of jealousy in their almond-colored depths. That she felt possessive pleased him.

He put his arm around her shoulder, dropping a quick kiss on her temple.

"No, Athena," he said. "We're newly married and need our privacy. I'm sure you understand. Is there no room at your father's resort?"

"There's always room for me there. I was trying to support you in your time of need. Are you sure I can't join your party? I've always thought three was rather fun."

"There are some things I don't share. My husband is one of them." Rania shot a death glare at Athena.

"Too bad. Call me when you get bored, Demi." With a dismissive toss of her bleached-blond hair, Athena strode from the hotel, her driver scurrying to repack all her luggage.

"Another ex?" Rania asked as Athena slammed the car door loud enough to rattle the glass wall in the lobby.

He didn't repress the shudder that swept through him. "A mistake."

Her eyes searched his for a moment. "I wonder how you'll classify me when we're through."

Before he could answer she pulled out of his arms and escorted the now registered family with the little girl to their suite.

How indeed to classify Rania? He was beginning to think that the mistake would be in letting her go.

Chapter Ten

Rania woke on top of Demetri. Again. It did seem that when she slept her body sought out what it wanted. Not that he complained. After a month of marriage their bodies at least were in rhythm. It was becoming hard to remember her life without Demetri. The restlessness that had plagued her for the past five years was gone. She'd found home in her husband's arms. They flirted and teased and at the end of each day made love as though there was no tomorrow. One day there wouldn't be. Until then…

She ran her hand down Demetri's side. His morning erection pressed into her stomach. With her ear against his chest, she felt as much as heard his words when he spoke. "I believe you could sleep through the end of the world. My alarm went off ten minutes ago, but I haven't been able to wake you."

"You could've woken me the way you do most mornings." With his hand between her thighs, bringing her to ecstasy.

"I didn't think I had time to do a proper job. You know I hate leaving things undone." It was true. He was a very thorough lover. "Now I'm late, so you're going to have to shower with me to save time."

She rolled off him and sat up. His gaze immediately went to her naked chest. Four weeks of seeing her breasts every chance he got and he was still fascinated with them. "I don't see how that will save time." Her naked body wet and soapy; his naked body wet and soapy. There was only one way the shower was going to end.

"Maybe not, but it will give me something to think about as I sit in traffic. I usually try to get to the office before it gets bad. Today I'll be in the thick of it."

"You could always work from home." She stretched her arms above her head and then quickly dived off the bed as he reached for her. Giggling, she ran into the bathroom with him hot on her heels.

"I got absolutely nothing done the last two times I tried it."

"Well, I wouldn't say you got nothing done. You did me at least three times."

He dragged her into the huge shower and turned on the water. The icy cold had her leaping into his arm. Seconds later she wasn't cold at all, and it had nothing to do with the water temperature.

"So what do you plan to do today?" Demetri asked as she lounged on the bed twenty minutes later, watching him get dressed for work.

"I'm meeting your lawyer for lunch to go over the latest developments with my uncle. After which I plan to get a few groceries and then get ready for the soirée tonight. Are you going to come home and collect me or do you want me to meet you there?"

"I'll have to call and let you know. I have a five o'clock meeting which I'm hoping won't take long. If it does, I'll change at the office and send a car for you."

"We might actually make it on time if we leave from separate locations."

He leaned over to kiss her goodbye. "We may be on time but I won't be anywhere near as happy."

Hours later, Rania wasn't happy. Another month had passed and her uncle was still in prison with diminishing hope of his release. In fact, the renewed interest in his case had prompted the authorities to move him into solitary confinement. So she couldn't even sneak a message to him via one of the other prisoners, let him know she loved him and was doing her best to get him free. The guards all appeared loyal to the current regime and were unlikely to accept a bribe to release him. And the government still refused to acknowledge they even had him incarcerated, as though political prisoners were a figment of the imagination. Amnesty International was involved but so far even with their clout they hadn't been able to get any relevant information. Rania was beginning to believe that dropping from an airplane into the middle of the prison yard and getting herself put into solitary was the only way she was going to reach Uncle Fouad. She was pretty sure Demetri wouldn't approve of that plan.

With a weary sigh, she got ready for the evening's event. Demetri had texted her ten minutes ago to say he would have to meet her there. Something unexpected had come up and he wouldn't make it home. She fingered the dresses in her wardrobe, finally settling on the provocative gown he had bought her when they went shopping together the first time. Although she'd told him she would never wear it, tonight it seemed the best option. Chances were once he saw her in it in public he'd whisk her home so fast she wouldn't have to stand for hours listening to boring investors talk about their golf game. Honestly, did rich people have nothing better to do with their time than chase a little ball around a field?

The car arrived on time and an hour and a half later Rania

swept into the ballroom of one of Heraklion's finest hotels. A hush fell over the semi-crowded room and more than one pair of eyes lingered on her longer than was polite. Maybe it hadn't been such a good idea to arrive in the revealing dress without Demetri at her side. Too late for that. She snagged a glass of champagne off a passing waiter and drifted over to the silent auction table.

"Rania Ghalli, if I were to go blind tonight I wouldn't complain that the last thing I saw was you in that dress." A man spoke in Arabic, so close she could feel his breath on the back of her neck.

Rania whirled around. Her first instinct was to correct her name. When her eyes met the smiling face of the speaker, she threw her arms around his neck and kissed him on both cheeks instead.

"Mahmoud! What are you doing here?"

"I heard you got married, and I came to make sure the guy wasn't a shit-head."

"You're here spying on me?"

"No, if I were spying you wouldn't know I was here. This is just a social visit. I saw your husband's name on the donor list and took a chance you'd attend."

"Well, whatever your motive, I'm so happy to see you, especially tonight. I need your help." She put her arms through his and dragged him out the open terrace door onto the patio overlooking the sea.

She had to talk to Mahmoud in private, and quickly, before Demetri arrived, because there was no way her husband would approve of her conspiring with an ex-lover.

• • •

Demetri stepped into the ballroom just in time to see his seductively dressed wife kiss another man before whisking him out a side door. He blinked. One month of marriage and Rania had moved on to another man. Rejected him. Or was this someone she'd known all along and she'd only hooked up with Demetri because he gave her the best shot at freeing her uncle? No wonder she hadn't objected to meeting him here. It had given her time to see her lover before her husband showed up.

His stomach churned and his chest tightened. Of all the scenarios where he envisaged their relationship ending, it wasn't a month after the wedding with his wife cheating on him.

"Demetri—" The voice of his most important investor didn't even slow him as he strode toward the terrace where Rania had disappeared with the mysterious man.

His gaze swept the patio until he spotted her at the far end, in the dark. She had her hand on the man's chest as she stood on tiptoe and whispered into his ear. It wasn't until his mouth filled with the metallic taste of blood that Demetri realized he'd bitten the inside of his cheek so hard it was bleeding. His fists clenched and all he wanted to do was beat the other man into a pulp.

"Rania." His voice was so harsh she jumped.

"Oh, Demetri." She raced over to him and kissed him on the lips lightly. He didn't return the embrace and forced his hands to stay off her body. He should never have bought that dress for her, or at least told her never to wear it in public. Even furious with her, his dick responded to her lushness.

Her cheeks were flushed. Guilt oozed from her pores. She grabbed his hand and drew him closer to her companion. "Let me introduce you to my friend, Mahmoud. We went to university together in Cairo. Now he's in the Egyptian military."

"He works for the government that considers you an enemy?" Even to his own ears he sounded like a pompous ass.

Rania laughed. Actually laughed. Although there was a nervousness in it he hadn't heard from her before. Was she scared of Mahmoud? Or him? Demetri didn't know whether he should protect her or walk away.

"Not everyone in the government considers me an enemy," she said.

Mahmoud stepped forward. The man was built like a tank; a few centimeters taller than Demetri, he was a formidable opponent. Demetri wouldn't step back.

"Mr. Christodoulou, may I offer my congratulations on capturing Rania. It's something many men have tried and none succeeded. You must be very special."

Demetri clenched his teeth together. He did not want to meet Rania's ex-lover, provided he was an ex and not still waiting in the wings for this sham marriage to be over.

"As my wife tells me, I was simply in the right place at the right time. Are you here to try to take Rania back to Egypt?"

"No, I am here on other business and our meeting is coincidental. Egypt is not safe for her. Please, keep her away. I won't be able to protect her if she comes home."

"Protecting Rania is my job. But thank you for keeping her company while I was delayed."

Demetri offered his hand, and Mahmoud shook it hard before disappearing into the night.

"Rania?"

"I know what you're thinking, Demetri. Mahmoud and I were at university together. I haven't seen him in years. And yes we dated briefly. Then he joined the army, and I left the country. End of story."

"Is it?" He wanted desperately to believe she'd just been catching up with an old friend, but he couldn't allow his desire to blind him to his wife's real nature. He knew Rania was an accomplished actress, skilled at manipulating people. The way she'd so successfully handled his family was proof. The lies she'd told about their first meeting had even made him question when they'd first met.

"Yes. There's history but no present and definitely no future. Introduce me to your investors, *azizy*. Then take me home and make love to me until the only name I can remember is yours."

She took his hand and led him back into the ballroom. They circled the floor several times and Rania chatted and charmed his investors. By the time three hours had passed people he didn't even know were approaching him hoping to meet his wife. From a business perspective, the evening was a roaring success. Personally, he wished he'd never come and seen Rania with Mahmoud. At least the other man had left after ten minutes. He hadn't once seen Rania look for him.

"Can we leave yet?" she whispered in his ear when they were alone for a few seconds. Her warm breath feathered down his neck making his collar seem too tight.

"Absolutely."

Even as they made their way to the door, a dozen people stopped him. Several wanted to know when he was opening his next resort and could they get in early. Bob Richardson, one of his principal investors, stopped them with a hand on Demetri's arm. "What about the exclusive resort you mentioned once on an unknown island. You still going ahead with that?"

Rania stiffened beside him. "It's under consideration. However, I understand there are several environmental factors that need to be addressed. I'll keep you informed, Bob. Now, if you'll excuse us, my wife is tired and wishes to go home."

The smile in Bob's eyes said he knew exactly why they wanted to leave and that a bed may be involved but it wouldn't be for sleeping. "Of course. Congratulations, on your recent marriage, by the way. I hope this doesn't mean you'll be slowing down."

"On the contrary. With Rania at my side anything is possible," Demetri said.

Bob laughed and patted him on the back before returning to the group he'd originally been conversing with.

"If there are more people you need to speak with…" Rania gazed up at him. The banked desire in her eyes made his mouth go dry. Would he ever have enough of this woman?

"Another time. I have more pressing needs at the moment." He pulled her closer so she could feel his meaning.

Her delicious laugh flowed over him, heating him further. Where to take her was the question. He'd expected it to be a late night so he'd had the yacht brought around to Heraklion harbor. He'd discovered though, during their recent sail around some of the islands, that sound traveled through the boat and across the water. And he preferred Rania's screams as she climaxed to be exclusive to his ears. There was always a hotel, but without a change of clothes he didn't figure she'd be too happy walking out in her seductive dress in the full light of day. Or they could drive the hour and a half back home. But that was an hour and a half he'd rather spend buried to the hilt inside his wife.

Then there was the consideration of Rania's friend, Mahmoud. He'd prefer to get her as far away from the man, enemy or not, as possible. Home it was. Time to put a damper on his desire and drive like a man desperate for his woman.

As soon as they were out of the city, he sped up. His Mercedes SL AMG hugged the curves as they whizzed past olive groves and small farms. With no streetlights he had to concentrate on the dark road. Yet it was the woman next to him and not the thrill of the drive that made his pulse quicken.

"What's your hurry, *azizy*?" she asked, her voice full of laughter.

"That dress looks uncomfortable. I'm sure you're anxious

to get out of it."

"It's not too bad, but you'll be pleased to know there are no buttons. In fact, if I release this zipper under my arm, it slips right off my shoulders. See?"

He glanced over at her and nearly drove off the road. Rania had taken off the top of her dress. The lights of an oncoming car shone on her naked breasts. He got the car under control and dared to look at her again. She was shimmying out of the rest of the gown. "Rania, are you trying to get us killed?"

"No, I'm trying to get you to pull over somewhere and relieve this ache between my thighs. Don't you know how sexy you are in that tux? It's taken every bit of my self-control not to do you in the middle of the dance floor and scandalize your business acquaintances."

A gravel road appeared on his right and he wrenched the steering wheel toward it. He wrestled with the car as the tires tried to find grip on the loose surface. Without daring to glance over again, he pulled into a small track in an olive grove and stopped the car as Rania tossed her dress and underpants into the back. She sat next to him, wearing high heels, a seatbelt and a smile that could melt metal.

What it did to his heart was beyond repairing.

What the hell has come over me? She'd worried about losing her heart to Demetri. Who knew her mind would go first? She'd had three glasses of champagne, but she wasn't drunk. At least not on alcohol. Yet here she was naked in the front seat of Demetri's car, demanding he take her immediately. Her skin tingled and she couldn't manage a lungful of air. For God's sake she was panting like a dog on a hot day.

"You haven't thought this through, have you?" Demetri said against her lips. He'd unclipped his seatbelt and hers but there was still the damn console between them. Her reply was cut off as he caressed her breasts and took her mouth in a torrid kiss.

He released her lips and trailed love bites down her neck while his other hand slid down to her core. She was so ready for him if he touched her, she'd come in a heartbeat. Where was the fun in that?

"Outside," she managed to say.

"What?"

"Outside. Now." She pulled away and opened her car door and got out. Her hair was still in an elaborate up-do, so she didn't even have that to cover her for warmth. She wiggled her toes in her four-inch heels and tried to appear like this was another regular episode in the life of an unstable woman.

"Rania, you're going to get us arrested." Despite his protest he was at her side in an instant. She glanced around. The area was pitch black, illuminated only by a faint moon and a million stars. You couldn't even see the main road from where they were. Grabbing his belt she pulled him against her. The cool metal of the car was a shock to her back. A breeze rippled over her naked skin heightening her nerve endings.

Demetri had taken off his suit jacket and bowtie before he drove. She undid his pants and slipped her hand into his briefs. He was as ready as she was. "Well, if we might get arrested, maybe I should practice the pose." Spinning around she spread her legs hip width apart and put her hands on the roof of the low-slung car, bending over so her breasts dangled down like low-hanging fruit. "Frisk me."

"Rania." Her name came from so deep inside him she felt the rumble against her naked back. He ran his hands up and down her body, tugging gently on her nipples before he freed himself from his pants and plunged inside her. She braced herself against the car as his thrusts increased in tempo, biting back a scream as she came hard. Demetri climaxed seconds later. The air was cold on her sweat-slicked skin, but she didn't care.

Too soon he slipped out and her knees buckled. She would have fallen to the ground if his arm hadn't come around her waist. They both froze as the sound of tires on the gravel road reached them. Demetri's brain engaged before hers and he quickly pulled up his pants and refastened them before opening the car door and ushering her inside.

He raced around to the other side and slipped into the car. The other vehicle passed without stopping and Demetri released a huge breath. "Are you okay?" he asked. She was covered in goose bumps and shivered in the aftermath of their frantic intercourse.

"Better than okay. You can drive us home now." Her intense need for this man scared her. How would she cope when it was over?

"That's it? Thanks, carry on?"

"What do you want? Payment?"

The interior light in the car went out, but not before she caught a glimpse of the anger in his eyes. "Don't ever do that again," he said through clenched teeth.

"What, take my clothes off in the car? I'm sorry, I thought you'd enjoy it. How stupid of me not to remember you don't like to lose control."

"Don't ever demean what we share and try to give it some monetary value." His voice was raw. "Get dressed. I'm going to make sure there's nothing unseen to hit when I turn around. Last thing I need tonight is a damaged car."

He flung himself out of the car and slammed the door behind him. While she reclaimed her dress from the backseat she saw him use the light of his phone to scan the ground for debris. Putting the dress back on in the close confines of the car wasn't as easy as getting out of it. For good measure, she pulled Demetri's suit jacket around her shoulders. She was cold now, but it was more from within than an external discomfort.

Demetri returned to the driver's seat and after a quick check to make sure she had her seatbelt fastened, he carefully turned the car around in the narrow lane and returned to the highway. The drive back to the house was done in complete silence.

Had she just pushed her husband too far?

· · ·

Demetri slammed the car into park in the garage and rested his forehead on the steering wheel. He'd let Rania off at the front door, opening it for her and leading her inside before he put the car away. He needed a moment to gather his scattered wits.

Rania had taken his well-ordered, planned-out life and ripped it to shreds. She pulled him apart with every glance, every laugh, every sigh. He'd had his share of lovers over the years. Not one had ever made him lose control so completely that he'd taken her in seconds on the side of the road like a barbarian. It'd been exhilarating and astonishing and so goddamned intense even now his body trembled at the memory. And then Rania had cheapened the whole thing by mentioning money.

Did their intimacy mean nothing to her? Because it sure as hell turned him inside out. Maybe it was just physical to her. Maybe she didn't feel the connection he experienced every time he touched her. Maybe he imagined the look in her eyes that said she needed him as much as he needed her. Not want, need.

He shut the engine off, closed the garage door, and entered the house through the basement. All the lights were off. Had Rania gone to bed? Which bed? They hadn't slept apart since they'd been married.

After checking all the lower doors were locked, Demetri climbed the cement stairs to the main floor. The cool, silvery moonlight lit the room from outside. He was struck by how stark and sterile the room was. It was like an institution or a clinic, not a home. The shack in Gavdos that Rania had decorated had more warmth and appeal than this place. Tomorrow they'd shop for some rugs to warm the place up, and maybe discuss color, anything but fuchsia.

"I'm sorry." Rania's voice came to him through the dark, startling him from his decorating ideas.

"For what?"

She stood against the patio doors, staring out into the dark night.

"For making you lose control. I know you don't enjoy that."

He strode over to her and wrapped his arms around her waist from the back. Dropping a kiss on the back of her neck, he inhaled deeply of her perfume. She leaned back into him and warmth swept through his body. "I'll let you in on a little secret," he whispered into her ear. "I haven't been in full control since you walked into my shower on the boat. I'm starting to get used to it."

He trailed kisses from her ear down to the collar of his suit jacket, which she still wore. Rania turned in his arms and rested her cheek against his chest. The jacket fell to the floor. "You should stop fighting it and just let go and embrace the chaos."

"You know I can't do that, not on a regular basis, anyway. And you're wrong. I don't regret tonight. It was raw and powerful and incredible. I'll never be able to drive that road again without a hard-on."

"Glad I could make a boring drive more interesting. Take

me to bed, *azizy*. Make love to me your way, all calm and controlled."

He swung her into his arms and strode toward the bedroom. "I'm going to make you eat those words."

Her laugh slid down his spine like warm honey. He'd show her that fast and frantic had its place, but so did slow and sensual.

Later, Rania lay on top of him, her body covered in sweat, her hair plastered to her back. "That was amazing. Chalk one up for control."

"This is why we make a great partnership. I'm enjoying this marriage, *agape mou*. Maybe it doesn't have to be temporary…" He held his breath as he waited for her response. The more he'd thought about it, the more he wanted to forget their agreed upon end date and make more permanent plans. Maybe even make babies.

Rania raised her head from his chest and stared into his eyes. "Spectacular sex is not enough to base a marriage on. For it to last through the tough times, there has to be love and commitment."

He swallowed. Commitment he could do. That was a matter of control—making a promise to someone and sticking to it, no matter the cost. Love was another issue. Love meant giving over your heart, your soul, to another person, hoping they'd care for it. Making yourself vulnerable to a world of rejection and pain. Love meant losing control completely, forever. He wasn't sure he could do that. He had to clear his throat before he could speak. "We don't have to decide now. Let's revisit in six months and see where we are then."

He could tell his answer disappointed Rania. She blinked several times and lowered her head to his chest again. "Do you think my uncle will still be alive in six months?"

"Rania, if your uncle is not out of prison in six weeks, I personally will go to Egypt and secure his release."

She raised her head again and searched his face. "If my uncle is free and you buy your land, what is there to keep us together?"

"This?" he ran his hand down her body and felt her quiver. She was always ready for more, no matter how often they satisfied each other.

"It's not enough, *azizy*. You'll see."

Chapter Eleven

"What the hell do you mean you're going to Turkey with my mother?" Demetri paced the patio, his hands clenched into fists at his side.

"I told you weeks ago that your mother wants to try to find your father. She's finally worked up the courage to tell your grandparents. And we think we've located him, so we're going to see if it's really him. Besides, you're traveling to Tirana next week to meet with the Albanian government." Rania stretched, hoping to distract her husband from his anger. He'd come home early from work and caught her on the phone with his mother while she sunbathed on the patio. His eyes flicked over her bikini-clad body but he made no move to approach her. Damn, he was in full control. It was hard to reach him when he had all his shields up.

"I expected you to come with me."

"I've been there, done that. Albania doesn't interest me. Plus, you suggested getting some rugs for the house. Turkey is the ideal place to buy rugs."

"Don't try to get practical on me, Rania. It doesn't suit

you. I don't want my mother to go to Turkey. I don't want you to go to Turkey. How do I know you won't try to get into Egypt? My lawyer tells me you call him every day for an update. I know you're frustrated with the slow progress in your uncle's case. The negotiations are delicate and have to be conducted with utmost secrecy. All that takes time."

"Time, time, time. Do you know how long I've heard those words? It takes time, Rania. Be patient, Rania. Sit down and let the men handle it, Rania." She leapt to her feet and stopped Demetri mid-pace with a finger on his chest. "Time's up. I'm done being patient."

Demetri grabbed her shoulders and waited for her to look him in the face. It was hard, as though sculpted from stone. She cursed the flutter in her chest at his intense expression. How annoying was it that all she wanted was to throw herself in his arms and never leave when there was still so much to be done?

"I asked you to trust me. I promised you I would get your uncle free. We are so close. If you go barreling in there now, you'll destroy the past two months of work. Don't make me force you to come with me, for your own safety."

"My safety? Or your pleasure? What will you do without your interactive sex toy for three days? Because that's what's holding us together, sex."

Demetri released her suddenly, and she stumbled backward, narrowly avoiding falling into the pool. His hands clenched once more at his side and he hauled in several deep breaths. When he turned back to her, his face was impassive again, which only infuriated her further.

"You may accompany my mother to Turkey on one condition. A bodyguard who I select and hire will go with you. If you try to get to Egypt, I'll have you bound and gagged and returned on the next plane."

Rania clenched her teeth together to stop the violent

outburst threatening to erupt. She was a grown woman and had been looking after herself for the past five years. What gave Demetri the right to tell her what she could and couldn't do? *A marriage certificate*, the little voice in her head reasoned. Damn voice. The whole object of the trip was to help Maria, so at least she could do that. And if she should happen to meet Mahmoud in Istanbul and find out how he was getting on in his quest, well, that would be an unavoidable bonus.

"All right, bodyguard and no going to Egypt. I think I can handle that."

Demetri still didn't seem pleased but at least his statue face had relaxed a little. "A package came for you. It was delivered to my office. I left it on the coffee table."

She raced into the house and ripped open the wrapping. She didn't need to find a return address to know it came from Mahmoud. Carefully, she pulled aside the tissue paper and released a sigh. Mahmoud was very clever. She'd heard a rumor he'd moved from regular army into intelligence gathering. This package proved it true.

"What is it?" Demetri lounged against the doorframe. His pose casual, his eyes anything but.

"A belly dance costume. Isn't it gorgeous?" She lifted the sheer, aqua blue veil from the package and showed him. There was a coded message in the intricate design embroidered into the delicate fabric.

"You belly dance?"

"Yes. I thought I'd earn the money needed to free my uncle by dancing at some of the local restaurants."

"You told me you expected it would take a shit-load of money to free your uncle. You plan to earn that much by dancing?" He straightened and walked into the room. Leaning down, he pulled the small, jewel encrusted bikini top from the box. A row of coins jangled as he lifted it up to the light.

"I'm very, very good. I make a lot in tips." She took the skirt out and held it against her. It was the most scandalous belly dance costume she'd ever seen. Sheer panels on the sides of the skirt from the hip to mid-thigh revealed way too much skin. No way would even she dare wear it in public. Mahmoud must have had a real laugh when he'd selected it. However as the entire purpose of the outfit was to pass a message, it didn't matter anyway.

"Show me."

Her lips curved upward in a slow, seductive smile. This would test Demetri's control. She took the top from his hand and disappeared down the hall to the bedroom. The three rows of fake coins stitched to a see-through panel of material were all that covered her ass and they jangled out her return. Demetri glanced up from the magazine he was reading and his jaw dropped open. He placed the journal beside him and sat up straight. Rania selected an appropriate song on her phone and connected it to the speakers.

The pounding of tribal drums filled the room and her hips moved in rhythm. She lost herself in the music—twitching, swaying, undulating and rolling her hips and torso in time with the beat. When the music became more sensual, she shimmied over to where Demetri sat. His gaze was riveted on her. Just out of his reach she did chest drops as though releasing her breasts from an invisible string. He sucked in a deep breath.

Another song came on, this one a haunting melody of a woman who'd lost her man. Rania let the Arabic words into her heart, and her body writhed with the singer's longing. At the end of the song, the lover returned and the song changed to one of exultation. As the last note died away, Rania stopped in front of Demetri. Her breathing was rapid and her heartbeat so loud she was sure he could hear it. She'd never danced that way before, with such abandon. Whether it was

Demetri's challenge or her new-found sensuality she wasn't sure. But she wasn't about to let him see how much the music had affected her. She'd let him believe it was an everyday performance and not an interpretive dance of her dread of saying goodbye to him.

"See, I can easily make 500 euros a night."

"I will pay whatever it takes to free your uncle, if you promise to never dance for another man like that. And never wear that costume out of this house." Demetri's voice was deep and husky, his eyes blazed with passion.

"As long as we're married," she said.

He swallowed again. "No. No other man. Ever. That is for me alone."

She stared into his eyes. "You have a deal."

• • •

Rania dug her nails into her palm so hard it would take days for the imprints to disappear. Natasha, the bodyguard Demetri had insisted go with them to Turkey, put her hand on Rania's arm to stop her from going over to Maria. They had found Burak, Demetri's father, but he didn't appear happy to see the woman he'd impregnated thirty-one years ago.

"You must let them talk in private," Natasha said.

Rania dragged her eyes from Maria's devastated face and turned to her protector. Natasha was pretty with short, dark hair and nearly black eyes. The only thing she'd said of her past was that she used to be with Mossad, the Israeli intelligence service. Now she was freelancing. Natasha seemed completely harmless but Rania had an inkling that if called upon she could rip apart a man twice her size with her bare hands.

Rania glanced again at the reunited lovers. Tears streamed down Maria's face as Burak handed back the photo of Demetri she'd passed to him.

"You expected a fairytale ending, didn't you?" Natasha said.

"Yes. My husband warned me this would likely happen. I was sure that once he saw her again they would live happily ever after. It was going to be like the film, *Letters to Juliette*. They'd see each other again and fall instantly back in love. Burak looks as though he'd rather return to the dumpster where he's lived with the rest of the cockroaches for the past thirty years."

"Real life is not like the movies. In real life, people use other people until they have what they want and then they leave. My advice is to enjoy the moment then move on with no regrets."

When Rania and Demetri both had what they wanted, would she be able to move on with no regrets? Even now the thought of leaving him made her stomach clench in knots. Would Rania turn into another Maria, unable to move on with her life, unable to love another? But Rania didn't love Demetri, did she? There was a fluttery sensation in her chest just thinking about him.

No, this couldn't be happening. She needed to get her uncle out of prison, secure the property for Demetri, and then get the hell out of town and on to her next adventure. That's what she needed, another adventure to take her mind off her husband. Her stomach didn't like that idea any more than the thought of leaving.

Burak pushed back his chair and strode from the small café where they'd arranged to meet him. Rania was about to go over to Maria when Natasha's hand restrained her again. "Give her a minute alone."

"You dabble in psychiatry as well as being a mercenary?"

Natasha smiled. "I have seen the hopes and dreams of many, many people crushed to dust and thrown to the wind. Mine included. Give Maria a minute, then we will go back to the hotel and you two can get drunk and engage in some sort of cathartic ritual which will begin the healing process."

Rania faked a smile. She was supposed to meet Mahmoud tonight and had hoped to slip out while the other two women slept. She could pretend to drink. The key would be to get Natasha to join them. "Sounds as if you know all about heartbreak. Maybe you could lead the party." And Rania would take careful notes for when her turn came and Demetri showed her the door.

A few minutes later, Maria made her way to their table, a tissue held against her trembling mouth. "Let's go," she said in Greek. "There is nothing for me here."

Rania put her arm around her mother-in-law's shoulders and led the way back to their hotel. A muezzin began the *adan*, the Islamic call to prayer, over a loudspeaker from the minaret of a nearby mosque. Having grown up in Cairo, the call was as familiar to Rania as her own heartbeat. Never had it sounded so melancholy before.

Hours later, Rania stood on the balcony of the luxury hotel suite that Demetri had booked for them. Maria had cried herself to sleep, and Natasha was practicing some type of martial arts in the sitting room.

Istanbul was one of Rania's favorite cities. Without Demetri, she had no desire to roam the streets, try the food, and find a little club to enjoy a drink and the local culture. And she still had to figure out how she could ditch her guard and meet Mahmoud in an hour.

It had taken her almost two days to decipher the message embroidered on the belly dance costume he'd sent. Finally, she'd worked out that the stems of the flowers were actually writing, backward, and in the dialect of her mother's Bedouin tribe. Then it became an exercise in memory as she tried to remember some of the stories her grandparents had told her and the words they'd used, which were different from the

Arabic the rest of the family spoke.

From what she could work out, according to the message, her uncle was about to be moved as there was too much interest in him where he was. They had less than a week before the expected transfer. If they missed that, then they would be right back to the start, not knowing where he was held. She couldn't wait any longer for Demetri's method to free Uncle Fouad. She and Mahmoud had to act now.

Rania walked back into the room. A faint crying sound could be heard from Maria's room so maybe she hadn't fallen asleep. Rania wracked her brain for an excuse to leave. "Natasha, my, uh, period started and I forgot to pack some necessities. I'm going to the shop across the street and buy some."

Her bodyguard straightened from the contorted position she'd been in and stood. "I can call the front desk and they will send some up."

"No, I'm restless. I need the walk, even if it's just across the street."

"I'll come with you."

"There's no need. You can see the shop from the balcony. I'll be back in ten minutes," Rania said.

"Do you not understand the job description of a bodyguard? Where you go, I go. Where you sleep, I sleep. Yadda, yadda."

"What about Maria?"

"She's not a flight risk. You are. Your husband was very clear in my instructions. I was not to let you out of my sight."

Damn Demetri and his thoroughness. Great trait in a lover, not so convenient in an overprotective spouse. "Okay then. Let's go before Maria misses us."

They slipped from the room and out onto the street. Music from a hookah lounge competed with the blaring of horns and the tooting of motorbikes as they negotiated the narrow, winding streets crowded with pedestrians out for an evening stroll. For a brief minute, she was home in Cairo again. She blinked back some silly tears.

Rania entered the tiny shop and pretended to search for the feminine hygiene products. A loud group of young men came into the store a minute later and Rania noticed Natasha became hyper aware. One of the boys said something to Natasha and while her attention was momentarily distracted, Rania pushed through the group and out onto the street. Natasha called after her but she didn't stop. Instead, she darted down an alley and into a café, plastering herself against the wall as Natasha ran by. Twenty startled eyes stared at her, Turkish men enjoying a last coffee with their friends before they went home to their long-suffering wives.

"Bad boyfriend," Rania muttered in Turkish before slipping out the door again and back-tracking the way she'd come. She was checking behind to see if Natasha had spotted her when she ran into the solid chest of a very large man.

Shit.

• • •

Demetri counted to one hundred in every language he knew. It did nothing to soothe his wrath. He was going to handcuff Rania to himself when he found her. He couldn't take anymore of this. He couldn't concentrate on business for thinking of her. When they were apart, all he wanted to do was be with her. When they were together, all he wanted was to tell her he loved her and beg her to stay with him forever.

But he couldn't do that either. How did you keep a butterfly captive and still happy? His life was steady, practical, predictable. Soon she'd bore of his routine and, as she'd said, even the incredible sex wouldn't be enough to keep them together. Neither, however, could he give up everything he'd worked for and wander the world like a nomad. He wanted stability, roots; he wanted a family—children he could love and tell them every day how glad he was to be their father. And he wanted to build a legacy to pass down to them. Unfortunately, he couldn't see having anyone other than Rania as the mother.

Therein lay the crux of his problem. Damned if he loved her, damned if he didn't.

The tinny sound of the public address system finally announcing his flight was a small relief. In two hours he'd be on the ground in Istanbul, and he'd personally search every centimeter of the city until he found his wife.

The flight felt like the longest in his life and when he landed, Natasha was waiting for him in the arrivals lounge.

"No word," she said without elaboration. He'd berate her later for losing Rania. First, he wanted to find out what she'd done to find his wife.

His first instinct was to pound on the door of the Egyptian embassy and demand to know if she was being held there. Natasha convinced him to let her use her network of associates first. Within minutes reports started to flood in: she wasn't in the Egyptian embassy or any of its known safe houses; she hadn't been seen at the airport, bus station, ferry, or any of the long-distance train stations.

Demetri stared out the taxi window at the passing lights as Natasha kept up a steady stream of instructions via her mobile phone in so many languages he lost count.

When they got to the hotel, Demetri was too impatient to wait for the lift and took the stairs to the top floor. Natasha slipped the keycard into the lock and together they entered the darkened room. A door clicked open and they both whirled around. Maria stood in a long, heavy cotton nightgown, her face blotchy with tears.

"Demetri, what are you doing here?" Her voice was raw,

and he rushed to her side.

"Of course I'm here. Rania is missing. I wasn't going to sit at home and wait for her to turn up." As far as his mother was concerned, his marriage was a love match; surely she would have expected him to come.

"Rania is missing?" The question ended on a sob and floods of tears followed. Clearly his mother hadn't been aware of Rania's disappearance. So why was she so upset? Obviously, her quest to find his father hadn't gone well. "Has she gone to find Burak?" she asked.

It was something that hadn't crossed his mind but sounded typical of his wife. Maybe Rania had gone to see his father, convince him to get together with his mother? If that were the case, she'd return soon. A flicker of hope warmed his chest. He'd been so sure Rania was trying to get to her uncle he'd never considered that maybe she was after his father.

He turned to Natasha to see if she'd considered the possibility. As she was shaking her head, the lock on the suite door made a whirring noise. Someone outside was using a key card. Natasha drew a weapon and took up a position against the wall and Demetri pulled his mother behind him.

"Rania!" He rushed forward to grab her when he noticed the man behind. Then fury blinded him and his arm fell to his side.

Before he could demand an explanation, Natasha spoke. "Mahmoud Hawash, I should have known you would be involved."

"Natasha whatever-your-name-of-the-week is, I didn't recognize you with your clothes on," Mahmoud replied.

"Get out, both of you," Demetri said. He strode over to Rania and touched her arm to prove to his unbelieving heart that she was real and safe.

"No," Mahmoud said.

Chapter Twelve

Rania had seen her husband angry but not like this. She knew he'd never hurt her physically, but he could tell her their marriage was over, effective immediately, that she wasn't worth the stress she put him through. Her stomach fell to her knees, which began to shake uncontrollably.

"I wish to speak with *my wife* in private."

Demetri was fighting for control, and the way he said wife sounded as though it wasn't going to be her title for much longer. Rania tried to swallow the lump in her throat but her mouth was dry.

Mahmoud stepped in front of her, between her and Demetri, knocking her husband's hand from her arm. "I won't let you hurt her."

"I will never lift a hand to her. However, I don't want an audience as she lies to me about where she's been for the past four hours."

"She was with me," Mahmoud said.

That was so not helpful. Rania quickly stepped around Mahmoud and put herself between her husband and her friend. Demetri would never hit her, but she was sure he wouldn't be so restrained with the other man.

"It's not what you think," she said.

"I seem to recall that was what you said the last time I caught you in his arms." Demetri didn't look at her; he kept his eyes on Mahmoud.

"She was trying to convince me to help sneak her into Egypt," Mahmoud said. Rania glared at him but her death stare bounced off his smiling face. Was he actually enjoying the confrontation or just trying to annoy Demetri further?

"And you agreed?"

"No, I did not. It's not safe for her there. I convinced her to come back to the hotel and let me handle the matter."

"It's none of your concern. I am her husband," Demetri said.

"Oh for God's sake, stop playing 'I've got the bigger penis,' you two. As far as I can see, neither of you have done anything to get my uncle free. If I can get to Israel, then I can slip through the smuggling tunnels into Egypt. My mother's family will help me until I can get to Cairo. From there with Mahmoud's contacts, I can arrange an assault on the prison and extraction of Uncle Fouad. We will probably have to lie low for a few weeks. Then we can either sneak out the way I got in or make our way to Libya and cross the border there."

"You'll be detained before you even get to the Sinai," Mahmoud said. "You're watched everywhere."

Rania crossed her arms. She wasn't a child. Egypt was her home, her people. She could blend in there, disappear without a trace. "I—"

"You will go straight back to Crete and wait with my mother. I will travel to Egypt tomorrow," Demetri said.

"And do what?" Mahmoud asked. "Your name is linked to Rania's, and you won't even get out of the airport before you're questioned by the authorities."

"Do you have a better idea?" Demetri took another step toward Mahmoud. "Rania is my wife and therefore her uncle is my concern."

Mahmoud stepped forward as well until Rania was like sandwich meat between the two large men.

"Boys!" Natasha's sharp voice cut through the testosterone-filled tension. "If we work together, we'll have a greater chance at success. I have the contacts in Israel. Mahmoud has the contacts in Egypt, and Demetri has the business credentials to procure the necessary commercial channels that will be required for a successful operation." Both men stared at Natasha. "I have personally led a dozen successful extraction missions. What's your tally?"

"None," they both said at once.

"As I thought. So I'm in command. You both do as I say or I will shoot you myself and leave you for dead. Any questions?"

"Wait. Demetri can't go to Egypt. As Mahmoud said, they'll question him as soon as he sets foot on the soil and then I'll lose both my uncle and my husband. The government knows we're married. They'll assume he's in the country to try and get Uncle Fouad released." Her heart felt as if it had been filled with lead and then reinserted into her chest. She couldn't let Demetri go. What if something happened to him? It was one thing to live without him because he'd be better off with another, more stable woman. Another to know he'd been imprisoned or worse killed because she'd goaded him into action.

"I can look after myself, Rania," Demetri said. "Besides, I have two resorts in Egypt. It's only natural I would check on them personally, as I do all my properties. It will be a legitimate business trip."

"That is good," Natasha said. "While you're making a big deal about your business trip, Mahmoud and I will enter separately and rendezvous at a prearranged location."

"No, I don't want Demetri involved," Rania said.

Natasha shot Demetri a look that he seemed to understand. He strode over to his mother and kissed her on the cheek. "Ma, why don't you go back to bed? We'll catch up in the morning. Rania, which is your room? We need to talk in private."

Demetri grabbed her hand and she pointed to the second door in the hall. They weren't even in the room before she heard Mahmoud and Natasha begin to argue in Arabic about the best way to sneak into Egypt. Leave it to the professionals; she had to convince Demetri not to go.

"You broke your promise to me. I've never been so terrified as when the person I hired to keep you safe called and said you'd deliberately disappeared." Demetri stood with his arms across his chest, his back against the door.

"I'm sorry, *azizy*. I was desperate."

Demetri stepped forward and pulled her into his arms. He rested his cheek on the top of her head, his hands rubbing up and down her back. She was home again in his arms, but she couldn't get distracted now. She had to convince him not to go with Natasha and Mahmoud to Egypt.

"Rania, when you're desperate you should come to me, not run off in some foreign country and meet up with an old boyfriend. Do you know how that makes me feel?"

She leaned back in his arms so she could search his face. The jealousy she'd experienced when she'd met his old flame Athena was clearly displayed. Coupled with that, there were still lines of worry etched in his forehead and his hair was disheveled from running his fingers through it in obvious agitation.

"I'm sorry, Demetri. I know you're doing your best, but it's not working. Mahmoud can make things happen. Stay with me. We can wait here or at the house in Crete, or even on Gavdos. I trust Mahmoud to bring my uncle out, especially with Natasha's help. That woman is scary."

"You heard Natasha—my wealth, my business connections, will be essential, and I have a legitimate reason to be in Egypt. The government won't dare hold me or they'll risk international reprisals."

"They've imprisoned one of their wealthiest citizens for almost a year. They don't care about their reputation. It's too dangerous, Demetri. Leave it to the professionals. Come home with me."

"Careful, *agape mou*. I'm beginning to believe you care for me. Or are you just worried about losing your lover?"

She punched him on the chest, but he caught her hand and kissed her inner wrist, his tongue making swirling patterns on her pulse point.

"I do care for you, *azizy*. If something were to happen to you… I'd never forgive myself."

"Nothing will happen. You'll see. I'll be back in your arms in no time. Then we'll take a long cruise around the Greek islands in my yacht. You, me, and the blue sea."

He lowered his head and kissed away any further protests. This time, though, their passion was tinged with fear. Rania poured all her pent-up emotions into every kiss, every touch. As Demetri entered her, their gazes locked, neither looking away until their bodies were spent. Rania wrapped her arms around his back, desperate to hold onto him, keep him with her.

When she woke the next morning, his phone sat beside a note instructing her to return to Crete on the next flight out. He asked his mother to go back to Gavdos.

For Maria's sake, Rania held back her tears. Her husband was gone. Would she ever see him again? Would she ever be able to tell him she loved him? Would she get the chance to try and make him love her?

• • •

Rania stirred another cube of sugar in her coffee and stared out to sea. Dusk was closing in. Soon it would be dark, and she'd have to face another night alone. Five days had passed since Demetri left. Five days of anguish. Five days of hell. She wasn't sure how many more she could take.

With no way to contact her husband, and afraid if she even tried she'd get him killed, she'd spent every waking hour staring at the sea, willing a boat to appear and deposit him safely on the shore. The soothing sounds of the water feature she'd had installed on the deck seemed only to echo her loss.

No boat came. Or plane. Or car. Was he lying bleeding out on the sand somewhere? His last thoughts wishing he'd just handed her over to the Egyptian agents who'd boarded his boat? She shivered and pulled the sweater tighter around her shoulders.

She'd downloaded from the Cloud all the surveillance photos she'd taken of Demetri when she'd trailed him for the two weeks prior to stowing away on his yacht. They'd played in a slideshow of regret across her laptop screen. She hadn't activated it in a while, so the screen was blank, like her life.

She plopped another cube of sugar in her cup and stirred. The coffee was cold now so it barely dissolved.

"I'm surprised the spoon doesn't stand on its own with the amount of sugar you've put in." Demetri's deep voice behind her was like a welcoming rain after a severe drought. His words trickled over her skin, bringing relief to her parched soul.

She leapt from her chair, knocking over the sugar filled coffee in the process. Her eyes scanned his form as he leaned against the doorframe. There was a nasty cut across his left cheek, and he held his left arm across his body. He was injured, his clothes were filthy, his jeans torn across the thigh and his shirt ripped on the sleeve.

"Demetri." Her voice failed her. All she could do was stare.

"I can't tell if you're happy to see me or sad you haven't inherited my vast fortune."

"How can you even think I'd rather have your money than you?" Two and a half months of marriage and he thought she was a gold-digger? Had he lost his mind as well?

"I have no idea where I stand with you, Rania."

She tapped her chest. "Right here in my heart. I love you, Demetri. I didn't realize how much until I thought I might lose you this week."

He straightened at her words but no declaration of love escaped his lips. She took another step closer. The warmth of his body melted some of the fear that had gripped her soul during the past five days. The aroma of man, sweat, and dirt was the best she'd ever smelled.

"I'm sorry. I failed. We didn't rescue your uncle. We were too late." He paused for a moment. "He's dead."

Pain sliced through her and she stumbled. She grabbed the back of the chair for support.

"I know you'd rather he was standing here instead of me." Demetri's voice was devoid of emotion, no hint of his own feelings. If he'd just tell her he loved her, or at least cared a little.

"No, I…" She couldn't choose between her uncle and her husband. She'd loved Uncle Fouad for decades, but it was a simple emotion compared to what she experienced when she was with Demetri. She didn't even know tears were streaming down her face until he reached out, caught a drop on his finger and placed it on his own lips.

"If I could trade places—"

"Don't say that." She'd grieve for Uncle Fouad tomorrow. Today she was going to be thankful for her husband's safe return. She reached up and cupped his uninjured cheek. The rough stubble felt wonderful under her palm. He was alive; she could ask for nothing more, except maybe his love. "Come. Let's get you cleaned up. You can tell me about it tomorrow."

Taking his hand she led him down the hallway to their bedroom. He leaned against the counter as she ran the bath, pouring in some soothing salts and healing essential oils. When she turned back to him, he was still completely dressed.

"The need to see you again was what kept me going," he said as they both stared at the other. She drank in the sight of him. He was home. Alive. Everything else would work itself out. It had to.

"You've seen me now. Is it enough?" She started to unbutton his shirt, careful not to knock the arm he still held across his stomach.

"Not until I touch you." He lowered his head and kissed her. It was the most exquisite kiss Rania could ever remember.

"How badly are you hurt? Have you seen a doctor?" she asked when he at last released her lips.

"It's just a few scratches, and I dislocated my shoulder. Natasha popped it back into place. It's still a little sore. And no, I haven't been to a doctor. All I need is you, and to sleep for a couple of days."

She'd make her own diagnosis when she saw him. Her Bedouin grandmother had taught her a lot about healing plants, and she kept a regular supply of essential oils. If it were anything more than superficial wounds, she'd have to convince him to see a real doctor. They'd figure something out to explain why he was so busted up.

She undid the rest of the buttons and removed his shirt from his uninjured arm first then slid it around and off his bad side. His shoulder was hideously bruised but the skin wasn't broken and the shoulder was in line with the other one. There were several minor cuts on his chest and his ribs were bruised as well. She ran her fingers gently over them but none appeared broken and he didn't flinch. In the mirror she could see nasty gravel rash on his back, as if he'd been dragged along the road. Rania shuddered. She'd done this to him with her futile quest to free her uncle.

"If you're queasy, I can bathe myself."

"I'm not feeling queasy. I'm feeling guilty."

He put his hands over hers on his belt buckle, stilling them. "I made my own decision to go. You didn't force me. You're not responsible."

"If I hadn't badgered you, if I hadn't gone behind your back and involved Mahmoud. I should have waited for you to do things your way."

A tear dropped onto their conjoined hands.

"Then I guess this isn't the time to tell you it was the most amazing experience of my life, outside of making love to you, of course. Not one I'd want to repeat, mind you, but not one I regret. Although I wish the outcome had been different."

"Demetri." Her voice broke on his name, her throat so tight no other words would form.

"I'm fine. Just extremely tired."

She nodded, unable to talk. Her heart was numb. She helped him remove the rest of his clothes and then he eased himself into the water. Carefully, she cleaned his wounds and after he dried off, she covered them in salve.

"Are you hungry? Can I get you something to eat?"

"No, I only want to go to bed."

She flung back the sheets and piled the pillows against the headboard. Demetri climbed in and she gently tucked the blankets around him.

"Lay beside me. I need to know you're here."

She quickly stripped off her clothes and climbed in next to him, careful not to hit any of his injuries. Demetri's deep, rhythmic breathing told her he'd already fallen asleep. She eased away and wept for her uncle.

• • •

Every bloody part of him ached. What didn't ache burned. He tried to shift to his side, but the sharp stab of pain sent him back to his original position. He must have moaned or made some other noise because Rania sat up. The moonlight through the open curtains illuminated her concerned face, blotchy from crying.

Demetri's heart fluttered. She'd said she loved him, and given her reaction to his return, he was pretty sure she did. So why hadn't he said it back to her? The last five days had proved to him that life is uncertain; you had to seize the moment. But Mahmoud's words still rattled in his brain. As Natasha had tended to both their wounds, Mahmoud had commented that Rania had certainly chosen the right man for the job. Thinking Mahmoud meant himself, Demetri had stiffened. Then the Egyptian implied that Rania hadn't randomly chosen Demetri's boat because it was headed in the right direction. Rather she'd done extensive research and decided Demetri had the money and connections to free her uncle. And she'd been right. His connections and wealth had been key in arranging her uncle's extraction.

Marriage had been his choice, hadn't it? But according to Mahmoud, Rania was a very skilled manipulator, getting people to do what she wanted, all the while believing it was their idea. Mahmoud himself could be executed for treason for what he'd done. Yet he hadn't been able to deny Rania when she'd asked for his help.

Another tear fell from Rania's eye but she quickly swiped it away. What would she say when she found out Demetri had lied to her and her uncle wasn't dead? In fact, Fouad was recovering from malnutrition, dehydration, and a host of other ailments under the tender care of Demetri's mother in the pink goat shack.

Would Rania understand it was for her uncle's safety that he'd lied? If he told her the truth, she'd undoubtedly rush off to see Fouad for herself and put them all in jeopardy again. They'd been lucky to escape with their lives. Until the Egyptian government truly believed Fouad dead, they had to act like he was. Rania's believable grief would help in the deception. Still, it hurt to see her so distressed.

Mahmoud and Natasha were making their way from Libya to Morocco. Despite a rocky start, they seemed to have clicked on more than a professional level. At least he didn't have to worry about the Egyptian man hanging around Rania when that man's hands were full of a trained mercenary.

"Are you okay? Can I get you anything?" Rania's soft voice reminded him of what he did have. For now.

As long as he was still married… "Just you."

"You're injured."

"Then you'd better be gentle with me." He flung back the sheet so she could see his dick standing at attention, waiting for her.

"I'm pretty sure this is against medical advice," she whispered but straddled his thighs nonetheless. She touched him carefully, almost reverentially, and when she guided him into her heat they both released a moan of contentment. This was where he was meant to be. How was he ever going to let her go?

"I think this is exactly what the doctor ordered. Besides, if I'm going to die, I want to go out on a wave of ecstasy being ridden by my woman." A faint smile curved Rania's lips as he quoted back her words. He closed his eyes as she began to move on him, reveling in every sensation. Too soon he spiraled out of control and went over the edge. His wife was barely breathing heavy.

Yet of all the times they'd made love, all the ways—frantic, tantric, playful, intense—this had been the most emotional. Or maybe it was his exhaustion and near-death experience that was sending burning arrows into his chest. *Tell her, tell her you love her and can't function without her. But how can I keep a butterfly happy if I trap her in a boring cage?*

"Can you tell me what happened?" Rania lay curved against his somewhat good side. With her finger she traced lazy patterns over his chest. He sucked in a deep breath.

"Are you sure you want to know?"

"I think not knowing will be worse."

"We did everything we could, Rania. Natasha and Mahmoud bribed as many guards as could be bought and we set up a huge diversion when they were moving Fouad to another prison. Then, when the time was right, we attacked. Your uncle was very weak, he couldn't walk so we took turns carrying him. We'd almost reached safety when the bullets started to fly."

"Was Uncle Fouad shot?" Her finger stilled on his chest.

"No, Mahmoud was. We got Fouad into the transport. Then he had a heart attack in the vehicle. I tried my best to do CPR but he slipped away."

"I know you did your best, *azizy*. I just wish I could have told him how much I loved him. How much I appreciated that he let me be me and never tried to force me into some preconceived notion of what an Arab woman should be like."

Fouad hadn't tried to clip her wings or keep her trapped. He'd helped her to fly and that's why she loved him. If Demetri tried to keep her with him, would her love turn to resentment? Would he see her spirit die a little more each day? He couldn't bear for that to happen.

He drew in a shuddering breath, his chest tight but not from his injuries. "I told him, *agape mou*. I told him how much you cared, that you risked your own safety for him. He knew."

A couple of more tears escaped and wet his shoulder. She kissed away the dampness. After a moment she swallowed, although her voice was still raw when she asked, "What about Mahmoud. Is he okay?"

It's just concern for a friend. "He's fine. Natasha dug the bullet out. Last I saw them they were headed south." Another lie. They were piling up. But he'd promised Mahmoud and Natasha that he'd keep their destination secret.

"And Uncle Fouad's body?"

"We left it with your mother's family. They promised to bury him near your aunt. Rania, it's too dangerous for you or any of your family to go get him. You have to let it be now."

"I will. Uncle Fouad is gone. I almost lost you. I won't risk anyone else." She resumed caressing his chest and he relaxed. They'd go on a second honeymoon, sailing around the Greek isles, visiting his resorts. Then in a few weeks, when Mahmoud and Natasha said it was safe, he'd take her to Gavdos to be reunited with her uncle, and she'd forgive his lies. Then she'd be so in love with him she'd agree to stay married to him, have his babies, and make wild, passionate love to him well into his eightieth year.

Yeah, right. And I'll also be crowned the King of Greece. Or maybe, as I'm half Turkish, Sultan of the Ottoman Empire.

Chapter Thirteen

Demetri stretched on the lounger on the deck of his yacht. The gentle winter sun felt wonderful against his healing skin. Although with Rania's careful tending, it hadn't bothered him much at all in the past two weeks. Not a lot had bothered him, including when he'd discovered the sale of the property on Gavdos hadn't gone through yet, because it meant he had a legitimate excuse to stay married to Rania. How long could he string this out? The need for the resort was dwindling. He no longer cared what his grandfather thought of him. There were more important people in his life.

"Demetri, have you heard from your mother recently? I tried to call her yesterday and your grandmother said she's gone on holiday. I'm worried Maria's more upset about your father than she let on."

"She's fine. I spoke with her on Wednesday. She's taking some time to figure out what she wants from life. You were right. Now that she's no longer waiting for *him*, she feels free to leave Gavdos."

"Did you just say I was right?" She sat up on her lounger,

a small smile playing about her lips. She hadn't mentioned her uncle since they'd boarded the boat a week after his return from Egypt. She probably didn't want to remind him of his failure. He knew she was still grieving; there was a melancholy about her that was at odds with her vibrant personality. And when she didn't think he was watching, she let the tears fall. He'd held her all last week as she'd cried, never knowing so many tears could come from one woman.

A thousand times already he'd had to stop himself from telling her Fouad was alive and doing well, just like a thousand times he'd stopped himself from telling her he loved her. He didn't know if he could trust that she'd stay with him. Until then, he'd keep his emotions to himself. He wasn't going to add to her list of hopelessly devoted men. In reality, he was at the top.

"You were right, in this instance. And when you climbed into my shower to avoid the gunmen. That was an inspired decision." His reminder of their meeting only received a tiny, tight smile. He reached over and took her hand in his, toying with the rings on her finger—the symbol of their union.

"Where are we heading?" She put her feet on the deck and stared at him.

Based on the intensity of her gaze, she wasn't asking about a geographic location. He stalled for time. "My resort on Santorini. It's my most luxurious and you haven't seen it yet. I'm thinking of expanding and wanted your thoughts on the environmental impact."

"I meant personally. Where are we going in this marriage? Are we still on schedule to split once you've got the land?"

A cloud crossed the sun but that wasn't what sent the chill through him. "I'm happy to continue as we are, even after the deal goes through. We make a good team."

She pulled her hand free of his. "Sex isn't enough for me. I've told you before; it's not going to hold us together when things get rough."

"Amazing sex, you mean. And I do care for you, Rania. You think I'd put my life at risk for just anyone?"

"You didn't go to Egypt because you love me. That was a pissing match between you and Mahmoud. You couldn't bear the thought that maybe he was more of a man than you, that he could get done what you couldn't." There was a definite bitterness in her voice. She grabbed her wrap and stood. "Going into danger isn't what defines a man. A real man isn't afraid to admit his feelings."

"A real man doesn't like being manipulated."

"What the hell is that supposed to mean? Newsflash, this marriage was your idea. In fact, I seem to recall you saying you'd turn me over to the Egyptians if I didn't marry you."

"You produced the Albanian marriage certificate."

"And you consider that a manipulation? Do you even know the meaning of the word?"

"Mahmoud said—"

"Wait, you're basing your judgment of me on something that lying snake said? Let me tell you about your new BFF. Mahmoud is an adrenaline junkie. He enjoys the chase, but once he's caught something he loses interest. He pursued me all through university, then once I gave in to his charms he cut me loose. So, yes, I used him, the same as he used me. I played on any lingering sentiments he had and goaded him into doing something about my uncle. If you recall, I didn't want you to go."

"Because you love me? Or because with Uncle Fouad gone I'm your ticket to an easier life? Is that what you're worried about, Rania? That this marriage will be over and thanks to the pre-nup you signed without even reading you'll be left penniless?"

She spewed a string of words in Arabic, which he assumed were expletives. "We've been married for three months and you still think I'm a gold-digger? Everything comes down to money with you, doesn't it? I don't give a rat's ass about your money. That's why I didn't read the pre-nup. I'll walk out of this marriage with what I brought in—a satchel of cheap clothes and my amazing ability to manipulate men. If you'll excuse me, I'm going to Skype with my family. Spend some time with people who actually love me." She turned on her heel and strode through to the cabin.

Demetri tried to relax again but he was too tense. He should find his wife and apologize. She was grieving and he'd accused her of horrible things based solely on his feelings of inadequacy. She was right. He'd gone to Egypt to prove he was as good as her former lover and therefore worthy of her.

When he entered the lounge, Rania wasn't there. Her laptop sat abandoned on the table, the screen open. He was about to walk by and look for her in their stateroom when a photo of him flashed on to the screen. Not a recent one, taken during their marriage, but from before they'd met. Another picture scrolled across, this one of him leaving his office building in Athens. He'd never taken her there. Mesmerized, he stared at the screen as photo after photo of him, over a period of two weeks, including the four days in Albania, flitted across the laptop screen. She even had a photo of him helping the old lady in Tirana retrieve her groceries, which had been strewn across the sidewalk.

Rania had had him under surveillance. She'd lied from the start. Her stowing away on his boat wasn't by coincidence and because she'd heard he was going where she wanted to be. She'd deliberately chosen *him* for his money and connections, and for being a soft touch when it came to women in difficulty. The chill he'd experienced on deck intensified. Finally he dragged his eyes away from the screen only to have a *blip* noise bring them back. A small message showed at the bottom of the screen. *Re: Purchase of land on Gavdos.*

Demetri hadn't involved Rania in any of the discussions with the landowner, knowing she didn't agree with his plans for the property. In fact, he'd begun to have second thoughts about building a resort there. As she'd said, it would make a fabulous family home. He'd even started to picture their children frolicking on the beach where he'd played as a child. Until he'd been rejected by his grandfather and exiled, that was. He clicked on the email icon and read the opening paragraph before a red haze appeared before his eyes and he couldn't read anymore. Rania had undermined his deal and was purchasing the property herself, through some family business.

Manipulating him into marriage wasn't enough. Now she was stealing his land as well. She must have been the one to let slip that he wanted to build a resort. His wife had a lot to answer for. He glanced up at the sound of a gasp and saw her standing in the doorway. A flush of guilt colored her cheeks. It took a moment before he could find his voice through the turmoil inside him. "Explain yourself."

Rania swallowed. Her eyes darted around the room as if mapping out all the escape routes. She opened her mouth but nothing came out. She was clearly deciding what story to spin him. He wouldn't give her the time to formulate another lie. "How long were you watching me?"

"Two weeks."

"Deciding I was the easiest mark?"

"Deciding whether I could trust you with my life. I was trying to get to North Africa. At first I considered going through Italy. I was going to try and get on one of the boats that bring illegal immigrants into Europe. After I watched those guys for a few hours, I realized I wouldn't make it to Africa alive, at least not without being repeatedly raped during the trip."

His stomach muscles clenched at the thought of Rania

at the mercy of human traffickers. Before he could comment, she continued.

"So then I came to Greece. And when I was at the docks, checking out private boats heading south, I overheard some men talking about your yacht and its maiden voyage to Crete. I didn't want to get into the same type of situation. So I trailed you for a few weeks to see what type of man you were."

"And you decided I wasn't going to rape you. Why didn't you simply ask me for help? Why go to all the hassle of stowing away?"

"Believe it or not, I didn't want to put you in jeopardy. I'd hoped to hitch a ride to Crete with you none the wiser. It didn't turn out that way."

"No, you showed up in my shower."

"Ten minutes ago you said it was an inspired decision."

He clamped down on his desire. He wouldn't let her continue to make a fool of him. "Ten minutes ago I didn't know the depth of your deviousness. You really are a scheming bitch." He gestured toward her laptop. "Nice piece of land you've bought yourself."

She swallowed again. All her machinations were floating to the surface at the same time. How was she going to explain this away? He'd expected a penitent look. Instead, she crossed her arms under her luscious breasts, her eyes flashing fire.

"I guess that's another thing I have to thank you for—in addition to saving my life—introducing me to the beautiful island of Gavdos. I wouldn't have known about it if it weren't for *your plan* for us to marry. Won't it be great? When you visit your mother in future, you can look down on your ex-wife's house. I only hope all the extremely noisy sex I intend to have with my masses of manipulated men won't disturb you too much." Without waiting for his reply, she spun around and fled toward the stateroom.

He stood and stared at the empty doorway. She had to

be bluffing. There was no way she'd build a house on the property and live in it after they divorced. No way she'd bring other men there and flaunt what he'd lost in his face. No way would he ever be able to go back to his birth island if she did.

It was even a worse rejection than when his grandfather had sent him away. He headed to the gym where he could work out his anger.

An hour later, Demetri had calmed down enough to listen to Rania rationally. He'd read the whole email exchange between her and Christina's uncle. The landowner had heard about Demetri's plan to build a resort and had decided not to sell. Rania had convinced him they wanted the land to build a family home, even sending him an artist's rendition of what it could look like. The house was amazing, one of the most beautiful he'd ever seen. It sat against the hill, almost invisible with its grass roof and sand colored exterior walls. It fit in with the environment beautifully.

He went down to their stateroom sure she'd gone for a nap as she hadn't been sleeping well lately. Her wedding and engagement rings sat on the bedside table. A stab of pain forced the air from his lungs. Rania was nowhere to be found. He raced back up to the deck and called to a crew member who was cleaning salt spray off the railing, asking if he'd seen her.

"What do you mean Mrs. Christodoulou is no longer on board?" Demetri glared at the deck hand.

"She went ashore as soon as we pulled up to the wharf," the young man said. "She only had a small bag with her so I assumed she'd gone to the market."

Demetri pulled out his phone and dialed Rania's number. The phone rang in the lounge. She hadn't taken her mobile phone, or laptop. Maybe she was coming back. The pit of despair boiling in his stomach intensified. In his heart he knew she was gone. The butterfly had flown. This was it, the marriage was over. Based on the intense pain in his chest, his heart had left as well.

If you love something, set it free…

• • •

A blanket of brown smog coated Athens' skyline. The Parthenon was barely visible from the luxurious top-floor office. Demetri missed the clean, salty air of living near the water. That wasn't an option now. He'd been rejected and exiled, again, although this time it was of his own doing.

He couldn't live in the house in Crete because it held too many memories of Rania. Ditto Gavdos. And the yacht. So he'd been forced to come to Athens and live in his flat here, sleep in a bed where he'd never made love to Rania in the hope that he'd manage to be unconscious for at least three hours a night.

His office door flung open with such force that it bounced off the wall and would have shut again if a big, meaty hand hadn't stopped it. If the Egyptian military were here to take him away for his part in helping Fouad escape, then he'd go without a fight. Prison couldn't be much worse than the hell of living without Rania.

"I'm so sorry, Mr. Christodoulou. I couldn't stop him." His secretary stood wringing her hands behind the huge man.

"Don't worry, Katerina. A tank couldn't stop Mr. Hawash. Please close the door behind you. And you can leave now. I won't be doing any more work tonight."

She closed the door and Mahmoud surveyed the room. Demetri poured them both a generous amount of whiskey before sliding a glass across the desk to the mercenary.

"You been engaging in extractions without me?" Mahmoud asked.

"No, why?" Demetri stared across the rim of his glass.

Had Mahmoud come to say that Rania had moved on, met someone else, and he no longer felt it right to be watching her? He took a long drink of whiskey, hoping the burn of the alcohol would anesthetize the pain.

"You look like shit. Cold, dried-up shit."

"Sorry. If I knew you were coming, I'd have put on my sexy face."

Mahmoud's deep laugh rattled the glass penholder on the desk. "If it's any consolation, Rania doesn't look any better."

Demetri stood so suddenly his chair crashed into the credenza behind him. "What's wrong with her? Is she sick? Why haven't you taken her to a doctor?"

The Egyptian laughed again and Demetri's hands clenched into fists. Maybe a good fight was what he needed. Get rid of some of the aggression pounding through his veins. And maybe Mahmoud would beat him into oblivion so more than just his chest hurt with every breath.

"She's got the same thing as you—she's love sick."

Demetri sat back down and took a large swig of his whiskey. "I think you're wrong."

"Can't sleep. Can't eat. According to Natasha they're classic signs."

"Why are you here, Mahmoud?"

"We're done."

"My money not good enough for you?"

"Your money is fine. We're recovered now and bored out of our skulls. Watching a sobbing woman wander around a garden, stare off into the distance for a while and then start crying again is not what I signed up for. I never thought I'd miss a firefight. Besides, Rania's leaving, and Natasha says there's no way she's going to Canada in winter. Where Natasha goes, I go. At least I know when I've got a good thing going."

"Rania's going back to Canada?" She was moving on. He had to find a way to do the same.

"You might as well give up. You're addicted." Mahmoud drained his glass and got up to pour himself another. Demetri passed his glass for a refill as well.

"I don't use drugs, and this is my first drink this week." He'd been careful not to turn to alcohol to mask the pain. It was hard enough to string two rational thoughts together since Rania left. Add alcohol to the mix and he could flush his company goodbye. Not that it brought him any joy at the moment.

"You're addicted to Rania. Trust me, I know all about it."

Demetri's hands clenched again. "I don't care to hear about your relationship with my wife." *Pompous ass.*

"Well, you're going to. Rania and I met in university. I chased her for four years until finally she agreed to go out with me. After our first time together, I realized she was not a woman to love and forget. If I didn't get out right away, then I'd be addicted to her forever. I'd already been recruited to join the military. Fantasizing about a woman while guns are pointed at you seemed the quickest way to a very short career."

"So you dumped her."

Mahmoud propped his feet up on the desk. "It was either that or die. What I don't understand is why you're fighting this addiction. You're not likely to get shot in your job. The only way you're going to pass away from a Rania addiction is if you can't eat because your legs no longer work from too much sex."

"It won't last. She said so herself. What I've got she doesn't want." Rania didn't care about his money. He'd always thought that was what would attract and keep a woman at his side. Take that option away and what did he have to offer?

"She doesn't want love and security? Doesn't sound like the Rania I know."

"She's a butterfly. She needs to be free."

"That's the lamest crap I've ever heard. You've got

Natasha and me watching her 24/7. How's that free? And she's miserable."

"I'm trying to keep her safe."

"Then stop paying others to do your job. She's your wife. Get her and bring her home. Keep her safe yourself."

Demetri finished his drink and poured another. The ache in his chest had begun to change to that fluttery feeling he associated with Rania walking into the room. Was there some hope?

"This isn't about Natasha getting jealous, is it?"

"I know how to keep my woman happy. And if Natasha were jealous, she'd cut off my balls, stuff them in my mouth and then pull them out through my slit throat. Loving a mercenary is an entirely different game."

"You really are an adrenaline junkie."

"It's how I live, but not you. And not Rania. Your adventures will be in making each other happy and keeping track of endless brats."

"I'll take your suggestion under advisement," Demetri said.

"Don't take too long. She loves you but she won't wait forever." Mahmoud drained the glass and banged it on the desk.

"Before you go, I have one question. When you met Rania at that event in Heraklion, was it really a coincidence?"

"No, the government wanted to check to see if your marriage really was legit. I volunteered because I wanted to see what kind of man she married, make sure you were worthy. The look on your face when you saw us together proved it. You were definitely in love with her, although you probably didn't want to admit it. Don't screw this up, Demetri. You'll never get a better woman for you than Rania." With a mock salute, he left.

If you love something, hold it tight and never let it go.

Chapter Fourteen

Rania trailed her fingers in the fountain, disturbing the water so it didn't reflect her face. She knew she looked dreadful. She didn't need to see it confirmed. Of course she could turn the fountain on, but it reminded her of the water feature she'd installed on the patio of the house in Crete. Had Demetri removed it, along with the rugs and lanterns and other knick-knacks she'd bought to turn the clinical building into a warm home? It could go back to being a cold mausoleum now, a testament to her husband's inability to love.

As promised, she'd walked out of her marriage with what she'd brought to it—nothing. All she'd taken were the wealth of memories that kept her awake at night—the sound of Demetri's laughter, the curve of his lips when something amused him, the touch of his hand, the whisper of his breath on her skin...

She managed a sigh past the tightness in her chest. This was her last day for lamenting the end of her marriage. Two months had passed since she'd leaped off the boat, almost as long as she'd been married. She'd finally accepted that the home she'd hoped to find in Demetri's heart was barred to her. It was time to find something to keep her mind engaged before she went insane. The job interview in Montreal next week would be a start.

There was nothing else she could do about her uncle's estate. With no body or record of his death, everything was held in stasis. She'd arranged for his various houses outside of Egypt to be maintained and closed down the few remaining businesses the government hadn't already seized. There was a pile of money in several off-shore accounts but she left those alone. They weren't going anywhere and she didn't need the money for anything. The only thing she truly wanted she couldn't buy.

She also couldn't stay hidden away in the walled garden of Uncle Fouad's Turkish villa forever. Turning away from the fountain, she headed back to the house only to stop after two meters. Her lack of appetite had caught up with her because she'd obviously began to hallucinate. A Demetri-shaped specter leaned against a column supporting the patio above. A ghost wearing jeans and a cream cable-knit sweater, a couple days' sexy stubble on his face. The tranquility of the garden was shattered. She blinked twice. He was really here, and he looked as dreadful as she felt. Had his injuries been more serious than they thought? Had he spent the last two months in hospital recovering and that's why he hadn't followed her?

Don't be an idiot, girl. He didn't follow you because he doesn't love you. If he'd felt anything, he'd at least have sent a letter or something. Even a goddamned text telling her to come home would have sufficed. She wasn't stupid enough to think he couldn't find her if he wanted to. Clearly, he hadn't wanted to.

So why was he here now? Maybe he had the divorce papers and wanted her signature right away. Probably had another woman in his shower he was anxious to marry, one who wouldn't take her clothes off in his car or procure erectile dysfunction pills for his grandfather.

She ran a shaking hand through her hair, unable to remember if she'd brushed it today.

"How did you find me?" she finally asked as he continued to stare. Okay, she looked bad but surely not unrecognizable.

"I've had you followed since the day after you left me."

"You had me followed?"

"Don't even try to play the outraged victim, Rania. You did the same to me."

"Fair enough. So you've known where I've been for the past two months. Why come now?"

"I heard you were leaving."

"And you didn't want to pay your operatives to go abroad?"

"No, I told you on our wedding day I would follow you forever."

"That was then. You have the property. I sent the deeds to your lawyer. I'm sorry I didn't tell you I was buying the land to give to you. Christina's uncle somehow found out about the resort plan while you were in Egypt. My sister Amal's husband is an architect, so I had him sketch up a quick house plan and sent that to the landowner to convince him to sell. There's no restriction in the sale deed against a resort. If you still want to build it, go ahead. You got what you wanted out of our marriage. Why are you here now?"

"I have something to give you, something I hope will delay your travel plans." He handed her an envelope.

She slipped an embossed card from the gold lined envelope. If she'd eaten anything today, she would have thrown it up on his shoes. This had to be the worst, sickest joke anybody had ever played. How could he be so cruel?

Her hand shook so much she couldn't put the card back into the envelope. Not just any card—an invitation to celebrate the marriage of Demetri Christodoulou to Rania Ghalli, to be held in three weeks' time at his exclusive resort on Santorini.

"Why are you celebrating a marriage that's over?"

"Two reasons. Can we talk inside? You look like you're about to pass out."

The lump in her throat had gotten so large she couldn't speak. Demetri put his arm around her shoulders and led her back into the house. She tried not to lean into his strength, tried not to remember all the times he'd held her, or led her into the house to make love to her. Focusing on the card she still held with a death grip, she pulled away as they entered the sitting room. Her knees no longer willing to hold her upright, she sank into the nearest chair.

"I'll make you some tea." Demetri left the room and for a moment she wondered whether she'd imagined the whole episode, except she still held the invitation to her belated wedding reception.

She closed her eyes. What kind of game was he playing now? He had the land. Was there some other reason he needed her to keep acting the part of his wife? She couldn't do it, couldn't stand next to him and watch him pretend to love her when she knew he didn't. A single tear escaped and she quickly wiped it away when she heard him return to the room. He had a tray with not only the glass tea set but a couple of sandwiches. Her stomach rumbled at the sight of the food, then rolled over when her gaze rose to Demetri's face. She still loved him. This was beyond cruel.

"What's all this about, Demetri?"

"Eat first."

"I can't eat until I know why you're here. If this is some investment deal you're working on…" Her throat closed up again.

He handed her the glass teacup on the silver saucer. The

sweet aroma of apple tea awakened her appetite. After a sip she picked up the sandwich and took a bite.

Demetri rose from the sofa where he'd taken a seat and paced between the chair and the patio doors. She took two more bites while he ran an agitated hand through his hair. Finally, he stood still, shoved both hands in his pockets and locked his gaze with hers.

"I lied to you."

She put the sandwich down. "About what?"

"Your uncle isn't dead. He's alive and well and living on Gavdos with my mother."

"What?" Rania jumped from the chair. Her glass of tea rattled on the saucer as she knocked the table.

Demetri took his hand from his pocket and stretched it out to her, then dropped it at his side as she refused to touch him. Because if she touched him she wouldn't care why he was here or the lies he'd told her.

"I did it for his safety and your own. We managed to get your uncle out of Egypt alive. I worried if I told you he was on Gavdos, you'd insist on going there and seeing him for yourself. We needed the Egyptian government to believe he died in the hail of bullets that accompanied his extraction. I wasn't sure if you were still being watched, so I had to tell you he didn't make it."

Demetri was talking like Mahmoud and Natasha now, discussing life like it was a commodity. "You let me grieve. You held me as I cried." He'd been so wonderful. That, too, had been a sham.

"It killed me to see you so upset."

"So, what's with the invite? Is this a ruse to move my uncle from Gavdos?" Oh God, she'd have to do it if it meant her uncle's safety. But to stand beside Demetri and smile and pretend her heart wasn't smashed to smithereens was going to take more acting talent than she possessed.

"It's more than that. Your uncle and my mother have fallen in love. They want to get married. However they can't invite people to their wedding because then it would get out that Fouad is still alive. So my mother suggested we hold a celebration of our wedding and invite all your family as they weren't at the Gavdos reception…"

"Doesn't your mother know we've split?" Rania fell back down into the chair and grabbed her tea. The lump in her throat was back.

"No, she's been living in seclusion in the pink shack with your uncle. Everyone except my grandparents think she's left the island. We've only communicated sporadically."

"I don't know if I can do this." She stared at the invitation so he didn't see the moisture in her eyes. When she dared glance at him, his face was rigid.

Demetri's hand fisted at his side. "There is a second reason for the invitation. But first I have a confession. There's something else I've lied about."

. . .

A flicker of anger showed in Rania's eyes. At least the flash of fury had dried her tears. "What other lies have you told me? You don't want a divorce to mar your reputation? You want me to live the rest of my life as the forgotten wife of the great Demetri Christodoulou?"

Demetri's pulse thundered in his ears and he couldn't breathe. The next sixty seconds were the most crucial in his entire life—his entire future. "I lied by omission. I should have told you long ago. I love you, Rania, more than I thought possible to love another human being. And I want to spend every day proving I'm worthy of you. I want our marriage to continue with you at my side where I can feast on your beauty and hold your hand through life's rollercoaster."

She stared at him, stunned. Her silence unnerved him and he fell on his knees in front of her.

He waited but still she said nothing. So he continued. "I'm so sorry I jumped to conclusions when I saw your surveillance photos of me. I assumed you only wanted me for what I could do for you. I was wrong. Is there anything I can do to make you love me again?"

She reached out and caressed his face. He was finally able to pull in a deep breath once she touched him. "I never stopped loving you. But is that what has held you back from admitting your love? You didn't feel worthy?"

"That was one thing." He had to lay himself bare, no holding back. She deserved to know it all.

"Demetri, *hobi*, my love, from the moment you rescued me from the gunmen you have proved yourself worthy. What was the other reason?"

"You're a butterfly, Rania. A beautiful creature meant to spread your joy around the world. How can I keep you happy stuck at my side? More often than I want, I behave like a pompous ass. I'm a control freak. You're a force of nature. You'll get bored of me and want to go off on adventures. How can I keep you happy?"

"By telling me every day you love me. When a butterfly finds a place where the weather is warm and there's plenty of food, it doesn't need to fly away. Each day with you is an adventure, Demetri. My home is in your arms. I want to share in your world, help with your work…create a family with you."

His heart felt like it had wings. For the first time in weeks it didn't ache. "Are you sure? Because I tried to live without you and failed. It was only when Mahmoud told me you weren't faring any better than I was that I dared come for you. I don't think I could let you go again."

"Then don't. Hold on to me, *hobi*. Never let me go. Keep

me safe in your heart, and I'll do the same to you."

"*Kardia mou*, my soul, you are the very essence of my life." He lifted her from the chair and moved over to the sofa where he could sit with her in his lap. It was going to be impossible to let her out of his sight for the next year at least. When their lips met, he poured every ounce of love into the kiss.

"You never told me the second reason for the wedding invitation," Rania said as she kissed her way over to his ear and down his throat. God, he'd missed her touch.

"I want to stand up in front of both our families and friends and tell the world how much I love you. I want to pledge my heart and my life to you. I want you to have the wedding day you always dreamed of, because this is the only one you're ever going to get. I have an event planner ready and waiting to fulfill every one of your wishes." His voice dropped and he nuzzled her ear. "I get to fulfill your fantasies."

She raised her head and stopped unbuttoning his shirt. "That was very presumptuous of you."

"Not presumptuous, desperate. Keeping busy, organizing the basics, is the one thing that has kept me sane as I wondered whether I was too late. Every decision I made was based on, 'What would Rania want.' It nearly drove me over the edge. I haven't slept, barely eaten…"

"Me neither."

"Then let's cook something together, have a nap, and then I think we can figure out what to do afterward."

"You always were better with plans than I was," she said as she climbed off his lap.

"As long as our plans include each other, we can't go wrong."

Two hours later, Rania curled up against Demetri's side. Her leg was thrown over his thighs, her arm around his waist as though holding on to him in case he was going to leave.

The gentle rise and fall of her chest as she slept eased the last thread of tension in him. They'd had to modify the plan slightly, making love before they slept. He was more than willing to compromise on that point. There would probably be a lot of compromises with Rania as his wife, but he was looking forward to the negotiations.

• • •

Rania woke with the most delicious sensation of being loved. Demetri had both arms around her, holding her tight against him. Through the crack in the curtains from where they'd hastily pulled them closed yesterday evening, she could see the faint light of dawn tinging the darkness with a pink hue.

Her stomach rumbled and the man underneath her stirred. Although they'd eaten before going to bed it had been fourteen hours ago, and they'd made love three times in that period. The hand on her back wandered down to her ass. Demetri was awake.

"Food first," she said as his other hand began to explore.

"Whatever my wife wants."

"Ha, can I quote you on that?" She raised her head to see a huge smile across his face.

"Today only. Well, probably more often than that, but I will stand firm on a few things."

"Such as?"

"First, if your nomadic instinct surfaces again and you feel the need to travel, I have the option of accompanying you. Second, you always come to me first when you have a worry. And third, when we argue, don't leave. Let me cool down and then we'll talk things through rationally. Then enjoy incredible make-up sex."

"I think I can abide by those conditions."

"Brilliant. Then let's get breakfast. We have a wedding to

plan."

Breakfast made, they sat side by side on the heated terrace watching the dawn turn into day. Demetri had one arm around her shoulders, he held her left hand with his. Rania was trying to feed them both from the one plate balanced on her lap.

"You know it would be so much easier to eat if I had both hands," she chided.

"I know but I can't seem to let you go."

She dropped the fork and stroked his cheek, the bristles from his morning stubble rough against her palm. He felt wonderful. "I'm not going anywhere. You know how tenacious I can be. You're stuck with me now."

He raised her left hand to his lips and kissed her bare ring finger. "We need to rectify this. Wait here."

Demetri returned a moment later with a small black velvet box. He knelt down on one knee before her and took her hand in his. "Rania, my love, my life, will you do me the honor of remaining my wife."

"Yes, I will." She leaned over and kissed his lips. "And I'll do you later as well."

He laughed and she reveled in the noise. Taking the box from his hand she opened it, expecting the jewelry she'd left on the boat. Instead the most incredible ring nestled among the velvet. Four oval cut yellow diamonds were set in the shape of a butterfly's wings. She raised surprised eyes to Demetri. "You bought me a new ring."

"The other ring I purchased for another woman. This is your ring. The yellow diamonds remind me of the gold flecks in your eyes, especially when they get bright when you're aroused."

"Like now?"

Demetri laughed again as he slipped the ring on her finger. "Whatever my wife wants. How close are the neighbors?"

"Not close enough to complain." Loosening the tie on

her robe, she spread the sides, exposing her naked body to the cool morning air. She wasn't cold for long however as Demetri quickly covered her body with his.

"Is Uncle Fouad really getting married to your mother?" she asked half an hour later when her breathing had finally returned to normal.

"Yes. I started to protest that they hardly knew each other. Then had to shut my mouth, seeing as I married you less than two weeks after we met."

"True, but how do you feel about it?" She snuggled closer to him, rubbing her cheek on his chest hair.

"I'm happy for my mum. I don't know your uncle well, but he seems a good man."

"He is, the very best. I never thought he'd get over my aunt's death. I can see how he would fall in love with your mother. He'll make her happy, Demetri. He'll dote on her and buy her everything she's ever wanted and tell her every day how special she is to him."

"Then I can't ask for a better stepfather."

"Do you realize if they have a baby it will be both my cousin and brother or sister-in-law?"

"Rania, I am pleased my mother has found love. I don't want to consider how that love is being expressed."

"You can say that while lying naked next to your own wife? I think you have double standards, *hayati*."

"*Hayati*, that's a new one. Another upgrade?"

"Yes, it means *my life*."

"I like it, but as much as I'd love to lie here all day with you naked next to me, we have a lot to get done. The wedding planner is waiting on the yacht. You tell her everything you want and she'll make it happen. Then as soon as we arrive in Crete, I've got a private plane lined up. We'll fly to see your parents in London and then your sisters in Montreal—"

"Montreal. Oh damn, I've got a job interview there next

week. I'm afraid I can't celebrate my marriage to you in three weeks, Demetri. If I get the job, I won't have vacation for at least six months." She sat up, forcing a concerned expression on her face.

"I was hoping to convince you to work with me. I plan to build several new resorts in the coming years and expand a few of my most profitable ones. I could use a good environmental engineer to guide me, especially one with such amazing vision. I also need someone to supervise the building of my new house on Gavdos. Make sure it's a warm, beautiful home and not a clinical, gray box. Or a pink one for that matter."

"Wow, competing bids for my employment. I'll have to weigh the options carefully."

"I enjoy a good competition. Mostly because I always win. Is there something I could do, something I could say, that would swing the decision in my favor?" He trailed a finger from her lips, down her throat into the valley between her breasts.

"Well, maybe there is something." She leaned down and kissed him.

"Excellent. Now, if we can move the rest of the interview to the boat, then I could make a start on selling you on my employment package…" Another package was already making its presence known.

"Oh, *hayati*, I love your attempts to get me where you want me." She pushed off his chest and stood, snagging her robe from the end of the sofa where they'd just made love. She trailed it behind her as she sauntered naked back into the house. "I'll do what you want. This time."

She quickened her pace as Demetri followed her down the hall, shrieking as he grabbed her and threw her over his shoulder.

This was going to be a most interesting marriage.

Acknowledgments

When I lived in London, the majority of my friends were of Greek heritage. Although an outsider, I was welcomed into their circle and was able to enjoy the incredible culture and hospitality of this amazing group of people. Thank you for teaching me to make dolmades, or koupepia as those from Cyprus call them. Sorry I never learned how to fold the spanakopita properly. But thank you especially for sharing your love for your homeland. I hope my book has done it justice.

A huge thank you, too, to Alethea Spiridon Hopson for loving this book almost as much as I do and for your brilliant editing suggestions. I also want to acknowledge the teamwork and support of all those at Entangled who make sure every book is the best it can be. I truly appreciate all that you do. And to Liz, my undying thanks for making authors feel like partners.

To my readers, loyal and new, I do this for you. Okay, well a bit is for me because if I didn't get these stories out I'd probably be medicated for constantly talking to myself. I already giggle loudly about random bits of dialogue that pop into my head at the least convenient moment. You have no idea how much I've laughed over, "I will not lie to my doctor to get sex pills for my grandfather."

Of course, none of this would be possible without the love and support of my family. The sign on my wall says it all, "I smile because I'm your mother. I laugh because there's nothing you can do about it."

Finally, to my support groups, the CR Sisters and my fellow writers at RWA-GVC, thank you. Your words of encouragement and understanding are priceless.

About the Author

Alexia once traveled the world, meeting new people, experiencing new sights and tastes. She's lived in Canada, New Zealand, Australia, England, and France, as well as spent time in Panama and Russia. When life demanded that she stay rooted in one place, she took to vicarious voyages through the characters she created in her romance novels. Her stories reflect her love of travel and feature locations as diverse as the wind-swept prairies of Canada to hot and humid cities in Asia. To discover other books written by Alexia or read her blog on inspirational destinations, visit http://Alexia-Adams. com.

Discover more category romance titles from Entangled Indulgence...

THE IRISH PRINCE
a novel by Virginia Nelson

Billionaire Aiden Kelley's life is flipped upside down when his ex shows up with a ten-year-old she claims is his. The only one who can help him is the one woman in his life, his executive assistant. Except she just put in her two-weeks notice...

A LIMITED ENGAGEMENT
a *Limitless Love* novel by Bethany Michaels

Racecar driver Derek Sawyer needs a fake fiancé to deter his sponsor's daughter, and childhood friend Lilly Harmon fits the bill. Lily used to dream about Derek proposing...but not like this. Money. Family. Love. It's all in danger if the truth gets out.

BEAUTY AND THE BOSS
a Modern Fairytale novel by Diane Alberts

Researcher Maggie Donovan has never had much luck with guys. It doesn't help that she's developed a massive crush on her sexy boss, Benjamin Gale III, also known as the "The Beast." When Ben finds himself in a tight situation, Maggie defies all the rules about office romances and announces she's his fiancée—jeopardizing both her career and the future of the company. In Ben's arms—and in his bed—Maggie's everything he could ever want...but if the Beast doesn't let her go, they'll both lose everything.

KIDNAPPING THE BRAZILIAN TYCOON
a novel by Carmen Falcone

Brazilian millionaire Bruno Duarte's plan was simple: return to Brazil and marry to fulfill his father's dying wish. But when his engagement crumbles, and he's then stranded with an idealistic woman so hell-bent on saving a tribe of people on his land that she kidnaps him, he sees the perfect solution. If his feisty and passionate abductor, Addison Reed, agrees to a bogus marriage, he'll relocate the tribe. But with the growing heat of their desire, will Bruno and Addison abandon their respective plans and give in to each other, or will their differences tear them apart?